I0649315

Morris M. C. O Connor

The prisoners of the temple

or discrowned and crowned

Morris M. C. O Connor

The prisoners of the temple
or discrowned and crowned

ISBN/EAN: 9783741185618

Manufactured in Europe, USA, Canada, Australia, Japa

Cover: Foto ©Andreas Hilbeck / pixelio.de

Manufactured and distributed by brebook publishing software
(www.brebook.com)

Morris M. C. O Connor

The prisoners of the temple

Quarterly Series.

ELEVENTH VOLUME.

THE PRISONERS OF THE TEMPLE.

ROEHAMPTON :

PRINTED BY JAMES STANLEY.

THE PRISONERS OF THE TEMPLE.

THE PRISONERS
OF THE TEMPLE:

OR,

DISCROWNED AND CROWNED.

BY

M. C. O'CONNOR MORRIS.

LONDON:

BURNS AND OATES, PORTMAN STREET

AND PATERNOSTER ROW.

1874.

PREFACE.

WHEN the Series of which this volume forms a part
was originally designed, a part of its plan was that
from time to time it should reproduce some of the
historical and biographical articles which had appeared
in past years in the Review with which it is connected.
Thus the second volume of the series, the *Life of
St. Jane Frances de Chantal*, was a republication, with
large additions, of some sketches of the lives of the
two daughters of the Saint, which thus grew into a
complete biography of their mother. The present
volume is of the same kind, being founded on a
series of articles on the life of the unhappy son of
Louis the Sixteenth, the tragedy of whose miserable
lot forms in some respects the most painfully touching
scene in the terrible drama of the chastisement of
the French Bourbons. Very considerable additions
have been made to those articles in order to render
the whole story more complete, especially as to the
lives of Madame Elisabeth and Madame Royale, afterwards Duchesse d'Angoulême. It is hoped that this
little book may now serve the purpose of giving a
succinct account of the expiatory sufferings of the
French Royal Family, the victims of faults committed

by their ancestors, the punishment of which their own
innocence, faith, and religiousness enabled them to
bear with a meekness as well as a dignity which
raised their characters to a level of nobility which
they might not have attained if their lot had been a
lot of unmixed prosperity. The writer has throughout
kept in view this elevating quality of Christian suffering,
as well as the action of God's providence, at once
judicial and healing, according to which the sins of a
royal house or of a nation are so frequently punished
in a manner to which the Scriptural expression may
be applied, that 'whosoever heareth it, both his ears
shall tingle.'[1]

H. J. C.

London, Feast of St. Francis, 1874.

[1] 1 Kings iii. 11.

CONTENTS.

CHAPTER I.

Causes of revolution in France.

No historical epoch is of more immediate interest to us than that crisis in European affairs which is popularly known as the French revolution. Every year increases our acquaintance with the men and manners which invited its reforms and explain its excesses. The student of the eighteenth century understands better and better, as collections of letters and manuscript memoirs are examined, that the collapse of the old system of society in France was no sudden outbreak of republican principles or communist passions.

The revolt of the people, in which yet lived some reminiscence of old Gaul, against the Frankish dynasty and aristocracy, cannot be limited on the one hand by the destruction of the Bastile, or on the other by the alliances of 1815. Some, at least, of the causes for that social disruption in France, of which no one can yet see the issue, may be profitably sought in the centralization and Court corruption by which Louis XIV. undermined the ancient liberties and moral life of his kingdom. The downward course begun by him had its natural outcome in the Regency and that shameful cynicism of manners, which was hardly so much the fault of the easy-going Louis XV., as the condition imposed on him by the vicious, coarse, and degraded

B

satellites who surrounded him. By the light of original papers, recently published, it is plain that the excessive blame passed on the predecessor of Louis XVI. is to some extent undeserved. Sensitive, affectionate, and possessed of Bourbon good sense and good nature, Louis the 'Well beloved' was keen-sighted, and, knowing himself powerless to avert the evils he foresaw, he sank, inert and discouraged, but not blind, into the slough of Versailles tradition. In it he grovelled till the end came, and death overtook him in all its grotesque horror and incidents, visibly charged with the Divine 'irony.'

The first act of the new King strikes the note of his reign. Seized with foreseeing awe, the boy of twenty and his wife of nineteen fell on their knees when saluted as King and Queen, and the cry was heard from them, 'Guide us, protect us, O God! We are too young to reign.' Let no one say that Louis XVI. began too late that effort at reform which seems to have hastened his doom, and brought his family, together with the monarchy, to a more rapid and tragical end than might have been, had he been less honest and self-denying. He was mistaken in his method, and weak in power of will, yet he remains a leader in those successive attempts at social reconstruction, which have been as remarkable in the history of France since his reign, as have been the crimes committed in the name of that philanthropy and liberty which he sincerely, if inefficiently, wished to promote.

The qualities of the great French nation have given a vaster and more definite form to the existing struggle between corruption and life, between truth and error, wisdom and folly, than is evident elsewhere. Its elasticity has hitherto restored it, after seasons of decadence, to fresh splendour. English invasion, Valois disgrace, and religious dissensions, brought it low, but only for renewed progress and the larger influence of its language and ideas. The sources of that elasticity seem now more profoundly affected than heretofore, and those who have honestly examined the causes of existing French weakness declare that for its cure there is needed a return to the old customs, and especially to those which secured family order, if the actual waste of national power is to be checked, and the people enabled to live on the interest, without exhausting the capital, of their strength. As it is, instability, from the government of the labourer's home to that of the country, is the main characteristic of society in France. The excellence of so many citizens, probably first in the world as generous patriots, does not avail to heal the war of classes and opinions. A double misfortune has overtaken the nation. Its natural authorities became corrupt, and in their corruption those germs of error fructified, which have wrought that worst evil of mis-leading pure and ardent minds eager for reform. It is not the vices of the governing classes, but the intellectual disease which those vices generated, that has so long hindered the revival of western Europe.

The doctrines of the 'Contrat Social' spread rapidly in a society which had lost the traditions of Christian life, and were more or less mischievous even in the sanctuary and on the throne which they were intended to subvert. The fatal falsehood, that attributes evil exclusively to forms of government and to imperfect social conditions, was greedily believed. The eloquent sophist who preached that the natural inclinations of men needed but free development to manifest their inborn goodness, was followed as an infallible guide to the Utopian paradise. Those scourges of society,

mistaken good men, set themselves to discredit the old·
ways and, in the poverty to which the Versailles govern--
ment had brought the people, the gleam of gold was·
distracting as the desert mirage is maddening to the·
thirsty travèller.   The hope of profit from a ' culbute·
génerale ' was a spur to the host of disorderly persons·
bred of social decay.   The new gospel of revolution
quickly spread from the drawing-rooms of bankrupt
princes to the workshop and the cabin.   Its leaven
worked differently as those in whom it wrought were·
rogues or honest, and perhaps it was most dangerous
in its effect on sincere and well meaning men, leading
them into moral entanglements from which the best
could not escape.

  The chief errors in the conduct of affairs, and which
seem to have most effectually weakened each successive form of government, appear to have been the
assumed omnipotence of the State and the steady
discouragement of family ties.   Unless the centralization of Versailles had paved the way for the first,
and its immorality for the second, these socialist
doctrines could not have vitiated, as they have done,
the excellent sense of the French people.   On their
appearance, popularized as they were by the charm of
Rousseau's eloquence, they were but feebly met by
teachers of Christiạn ethics, who were, and not perhaps·
undeservedly, less influential than they should have
been even with Catholics pious in their personal
devotion.   Christian ethics being respected only as far
as they were commended by the reason, it followed
that the superhuman mysteries of Divine government
were openly denied by all whose theories were crossed
by the immutable law.   Never did there seem a more
fitting time for a lesson to mankind, which, whether
it -were rightly used or not by that generation, should

remain for the instruction of society in less obscured
·epochs.

The sacrifice of Louis XVI. and his family to the
social evils and passions which his ancestors on the
throne had largely helped to evoke is, even when
most dispassionately judged, one of those historical
tragedies in which the Divine hand is strikingly visible,
and not the less so that in it is so plainly set forth
the law of expiation by the innocent of the sins of
the guilty. Sacrifice is the law of Being, and by it
creation daily advances in physical welfare, while in
the intellectual and spiritual progress of man it is
continually demanded. No battle is won unless the
bravest venture their lives ; there is no large evolution
of humanity without an expense of power that often
seems wholly wasted, no transfiguration of our nature
into somewhat of Divine greatness unless the sacrifices
called for be consciously and willingly made with
somewhat of Divine generosity. The life and death
of persons so innocent, so highly placed, and so
evidently victims of a nemesis they could not avert,
is surely, then, worthy of close and reverent study.

At an epoch when religion was, even by her defenders, made unduly subject to the limitations of
human sciences, when the millennium to be secured
by revolution took the place, even in sober minds,
of the Christian future life, there was enacted in the
face of the world this tragedy of the Temple and
the Conciergerie, a tragedy which remains irreconcile-
able with all notions of justice, and shocking even
to the sincerest republican, unless it be judged in the
full light of that revelation which justifies such expiatory
punishment.

All the greatest religions of the world have, confessing the imperfection of man, taught the uses of

vicarious sacrifice and the value in spiritual revival'
of the shedding of blood. The noblest societies of
the Old World are in accord, in highly esteeming
voluntary martyrdom as propitiation for sin. But
the history of the Temple would be the unbearably
saddest of all expiations, if those who suffered in it
and we who read of them were without the Christian
faith in future rewards, and had no knowledge of the
deeper meanings of pain, and of those supernatural
compensations which support and even rejoice the
victims in their agony.

The life of Louis XVI. and that of Marie Antoinette
occupy so large a space in French history, their motives
and actions are connected by so complicated a network
of causes and events, that a much larger volume than
this would be needed to explain their struggle with
anarchy and their defeat. Within the last ten years
a truer estimate of both husband and wife has been
possible. From their correspondence, when it has
been cleared of some fictitious letters, and from the
despatches that passed between Marie Antoinette's
mother, Maria Theresa, and her confidential minister
at the Court of Versailles, the Comte de Mercy
Argenteau, we get portraits probably more faithful
than could have been drawn by the most accurate
and well informed bystander. The more intimately we
are admitted into the confidence of the Queen, the
greater must be our respect for her; and, if some
pretty anecdotes and reported witticisms of hers be
proved apocryphal in the new light cast on the first
ten years of her married life by M. de Mercy's correspondence, our estimate of her shrewd discernment
and serious conceptions of her duty is singularly raised.
Without pretending that Louis and his wife were
faultless, indeed, acknowledging fully the imperfec-

tions of their respective characters, we can feel certain
that they were persons worthy of that corrective discipline, by which true martyrs are formed out of ordinary
human clay.

Count Joseph de Maistre observes, that when there
is collision between two parties, and when on one
side there are worthy victims to duty and conscience,
we may forecast the ultimate triumph of that side,
notwithstanding all appearance to the contrary. He
particularly instances the resignation of Louis XVI.,
and his refusal to rouse pity or appeal to aught but
justice in his judges, as an example of that voluntary
sacrifice which makes of the victim an offering for
others. The incidents of that unparalleled doom which
overtook the royal family of France acquire special
interest when considered from this point of view.
There is a fitness in its fate which is felt to be
judicial even when pity and indignation are most
excited by its story. The predecessors of Louis had
sinned by weakening local laws and straitening local
liberties in the establishment of a corrupt despotism—
Paris and its tyranny struck down the heir of their
error. They had sapped the foundations of social order
by domestic vice, which at once lessened respect for
womanhood and destroyed paternal authority — the
long agony of the Queen in her character of wife
and mother, the death of Madame Elisabeth, who
by her purity and piety had earned, even from the
rabble of Paris, the title of 'our St. Geneviève,' and
lastly, the living death and ruin of the Dauphin, are
set over against the special sins and follies which
made such retribution possible. It may well be hoped
that by so large and generous an expiation the victims
whose blood has been shed in France, during both
the first and second tyranny of the Paris Commune,

may win for the cause of religion and virtue its due
success, and that the long struggle between truth and
error, wise tradition and flighty experiment, may end
in restoration, not of the old forms, but of the old
principles and spirit which earned for the French
nation its legitimate influence.

CHAPTER II.

Louis the Sixteenth.

THOSE who write of the revolutionary Paris only as it
was an arena from 1789 to 1815 for the struggles of
particular heroes, or as it is a mere lesson in politics
variously commented by republicans and royalists, those
who look only at the terrible friction of its progress, or
who think of it either as a regeneration or as the fatal
termination of all that was best in French life, are likely
to miss the causes and consequences of the great up·
heaval with which our generation is mainly concerned.
To such the drama of the Temple is but a curious
fragment of the revolutionary mosaic.   But to those who
believe that the national crisis in which, for a hundred
years, France has struggled for life and health, is chiefly
traceable to the loss of family order, and to the substitution of novelty for custom, the royal sufferers are
otherwise interesting.   They are each representatives
of virtues and beliefs that cement family life, and of
the better and most vital traditions of France.   But it
needed reverse and uttermost humiliation before honour
and leadership could be won back by a monarch of

France. Energy, nobleness, kingly character, had been singularly wanting in Louis XV. and in his grandson and successor, but the Temple and the scaffold revived the obsolete virtues of St. Louis, the courage and generosity of Henry IV., on the throne which, sprinkled by a victim's blood, has not suffered the shameful decomposition of its rival forms of government.

Yet it is not as he was monarch, but as he was husband and father, not as the dull artizan of Versailles, crowned by mistake, but as he was strong and brave when there were no more problems of government to be solved, that we must respect the King. Louis Capet, as the servant of God, the pious and devoted head of his little household, is the living protest against those theories of the 'Contrat Social' with which he had, while King, the folly to tamper. The egotism and sensuality of the upper classes were beautifully rebuked by the expiations of the Temple. Good men who denied original sin, and believed that, once free of the 'ancient ways,' man must be happy and virtuous, might well be cured of their fatal optimism at the sight of Madame Elisabeth's murder, and of the destruction of the child-Prince, by malice of which no similar instance is known to history.

The royal family, united in adversity, noble, strong with the unconquerable strength of right principle, remains a witness to the social value of the Divine law by which they lived. Not when he convoked the States General and flattered the people was Louis kingly. He was awkward, dull, and vulgar in the purple, but in prison he reasserted the power of royalty as a social institution. There, birth and traditional dignity bore in gentle fashion the test of daily insult, while piety and a certain spiritual perception that the Decalogue was a law superior to all other laws, lifted the inferior and somewhat animal

Prince to a royal place in the sight of men. 'Providential equality' was rebuked, for surely in this family of discrowned Capets were providential superiorities, a nobility which none may question, a leadership in courage, faith, and love, which the believer in equality may explain away if he can, but which remain more eloquent than his theories. The inefficiencies of Louis, the frivolities of Marie Antoinette, bring in stronger relief the lessons it was theirs to teach in later life. Neither of them, however, as becomes every day more clear, had committed any wrong that could lessen our perception of the sacrificial elements in their sufferings. Another King might have controlled or led the storm which rose round the old monarchy. Louis might have more firmly checked the treacherous insolence of the courtiers led . by his own kinsmen, experiments in reform might have been more prudently attempted by a less conscientious man. When he began to reign he was without grace or dignity, timidly brusque, dull in manners, yet easily angered, fond of rough games and school-boy jokes, hunting and eating, yet not without the rudiments of those qualities by which he was afterwards ennobled.

A good idea of Louis may be found in a letter from the Emperor Joseph II. to his brother Leopold, published for the first time in the *Revue des Deux Mondes* for December 15, 1873. 'The situation of my sister with the King is singular,' he writes. 'The man is a little weak, but not stupid. He has ideas, he has judgment, but an apathy of body as of mind. He converses reasonably, he has no curiosity or wish to instruct himself, in short, the *fiat lux* has not yet been pronounced, the matter is yet inform.' Hardest of his shortcomings to forgive is the indifference with which Louis left his wife, during the first years of her residence at Versailles, to be the prey of calumny and intrigue, often indeed exposing her to misconstruction, and half countenancing the party headed by his aunts, and composed of all who disliked M. de Choiseul. It was the Court that first gave her that name of 'Autrichienne' which hunted her to the scaffold.

No one ever doubted the goodwill of Louis to his people. Pleased with a dozen fair theories, he had not energy to choose and act on any consistent system. No one has more signally exemplified the mischievousness of that muddle-headed philanthropy and futile desire for good which is epidemic among well meaning persons, but which is a powerful and almost resistless means to evil in the hands of the unscrupulous and energetic few who have definite and personal aims. Reverse and apparent ruin removed the King's unsightly weaknesses. From the day that he was finally clear of the pasteboard throne of Paris, which had been set up on the ruins of the old monarchy, indeed from the day in which, at the dictates of conscience, he faced his ministers and refused assent to decrees involving, as he believed, sacrilege and civil war, Louis regains his forfeited royalty—he re-inspires men with respect for the true principles of authority, and he is a model of that patriarchal dignity in which religion and civilized life have their roots. While the people without raved and went mad over a dozen schemes for national regeneration at any cost of crime and bank-ruptcy, the King, more kingly as the end drew near in lurid darkness, supplied an example of the virtues on which alone have races founded any consistent or power-ful nationality or prosperous commonwealth. Versailles had not been the place for their fortunate development, but even there the private life of Louis was an earnest of the future. Yet its atmosphere of poisonous intrigue was one that stifled healthy life. He and the Queen could not be their noblest selves, until the old existence,

its pleasures, its pride, and even the enthusiastic friendships, and innocent charities of life, into which Marie
Antoinette somewhat defiantly threw herself, were swept
away.

CHAPTER III.

Marie Antoinette.

OF the Queen, Marie Antoinette, what can be said in
short space that is not already known? It is no longer
necessary to show the falsehood of those calumnies in
which her brother-in-law, Monsieur, and certain parties in
the Court took so shameful a part. They have served
their purpose by obliging a close examination of her life,
from the day in which, not fifteen years old, she entered
on her difficult career as the Dauphin's wife in a society
of which D'Aiguillon and Du Barry were leaders, to that
when, noblest of the figures that suffered accusation at
Fouquier Tinville's hands, she crushed her enemies by
her dignity as wife and mother, wrung truth from falsehood, and pity from cruelty, and respect from official and
tyrannous atheism.

Even a slight acquaintance with history can sufficiently
explain why the daughter of Maria Theresa, brave, young,
and if not absolutely beautiful, as fascinating as ever was
woman who wore a crown, should have been a mark for
the arrowy venom of so large a party at the French
Court. The Austrian alliance, M. de Choiseul's policy,
was contrary to political tradition. The most capable
statesman of the moment, he was hated by a swarm of

intriguers and courtiers with whose schemes he inter-
fered, and among them ranked princes and princesses
of the royal blood, from Madame Adelaide, Louis XV.'s
favourite daughter, to the pettiest cousin and hanger-
on of the younger Bourbon branches. In estimating the
character and powers of Marie Antoinette, the difficulties
with which she had to contend have been hardly sufficiently understood, until recent researches exposed to
fuller light the temper of those aunts Adelaide, Victoria,
Sophia, and Louise, under whose influence the child-
archduchess naturally came. Though she had played
duets with Mozart and studied with Metastasio as her
tutor, she was of course but at the threshold of her education when she was required to take her due place as
the first lady of France, to be dutiful to her husband's
grandfather, Louis XV., nicely calculate the exact manner
in which to treat the reigning favourite, and steer through
the dangerous currents of Versailles intrigue without help
from her shy and unmannerly boy-husband.

Evil omens attended her from the day she set foot in
France. From the first brilliant reception and through
all the splendours of her early reign there is a continual
muttering of coming storm. The courage, sometimes
too recklessly defiant, of Maria Theresa's daughter must
have been royal in quality, for it has become impossible
to doubt, since her correspondence has been better
known, that the Queen had keen and shrewd perception
of her position and her surroundings. Those who
attack her conduct, and, ashamed to quote old calum
nies, make large use of some severe expressions in her
mother's and her brother Joseph II.'s letters, can be met
by other passages in their correspondence, as for instance,
after his journey to Paris in 1777, when the Emperor
writes to his brother Leopold, 'I left Paris without
regret, though I was wonderfully well treated there. It

was harder to quit Versailles, for I had become truly
attached to my sister, and I saw her sorrow for our
separation, which increased mine. She is a loveable
and worthy woman, rather young, rather thoughtless, but
possessed of a worth and virtue that in her position
merit real respect. With that, she has an intelligence
and clear sight which often astonished me. Her first
impulse is always right.' But the frank hardihood, the
ingenious honesty which she brought with her from the
homely 'Burg' at Vienna, were dangerous at Versailles,
where the corrupt and tottering monarchy was chiefly
propped by etiquette and traditional ceremonial. The
Queen's affectionate and outspoken nature, thwarted and
misunderstood as it was in the first year of her married
life, sought friends and found only favourites, who
wrought her far-reaching mischief, not yet indeed ex-
hausted. It was hereditary in the daughter of Maria
Theresa to sympathize with the people, rather than with
the stiff and insincere chiefs of her Court, even when as
respectable as were Mesdames de Mailly and de Marsan.
To their surprise, she not only declared that the working
men had 'hidden virtues, and were true souls capable of
the highest Christian perfection,' but she thirsted for the
love and sympathy of the poor, and, as far as was
possible, broke down the barriers that shut them out
from the governing class. It was not her fault, but that
of the nobles, who ran away and left her to the fate they
had prepared for her by their calumnies, that one day
she should be shut in by the people within that fatal
Tuileries garden that was nicknamed 'Terre de Coblentz.'
Her liberal sympathies were but another danger to her.
She yielded a too ready ear, if not to the prose, to the
epigrams of the popular philosophy. In this as in other
mistakes she erred, however, by the defects of her
qualities rather than by any vice of character or moral

fault. No one need affect to treat the Queen's follies of
Marly and the Trianon as not seriously injurious to her.
To act Atalanta in a gauze dress, to find amusement in
public masquerades, to play practical jokes on the King,
to trust her brothers-in-law, to smile behind her fan at
the venerable hags who attended her Court, or to throw
her arms round the neck of her friend Madame de
Polignac, were the heighth of imprudence in a society
trained to the worst construction by a hundred years of
profligate living and compensative etiquette.

To explain minutely the scandal in which the Queen
and Cardinal de Rohan, Cagliostro the charlatan,
and a female adventuress, were brought together in an
accusation of theft, is outside the limits of this book,
yet the fact that such a scandal could be possible is
evidence of the profound corruption at Versailles. Louis
de Rohan, a Prince of the Church and of the first family
of the aristocracy, was by the King's orders tried by the
Parliament of Paris. Before a scoffing and curious
Europe the Queen's pretended share in his profligate
extravagance was investigated. She was accused, in a
hundred libels of the hour, of making away with certain
important diamonds which the Cardinal believed she had
accepted privately from him. And when Louis de Rohan
was acquitted, she remained the victim of a false accusation that clung and still clings to her in the pages of
writers who desire to justify the men by whom her death
was finally compassed. Royalty in France never recovered
the blow. The affair of the diamond necklace occurred
in 1785, and within four years, in 1789, were enunciated,
amid general rejoicing, those principles which have
since been the gospel of revolution.

Doubtless Marie Antoinette's rashness made such
calumnies cling. It gave point to Beaumarchais' satire,
and to Monsieur's insinuations. It was but the result of

her frank impatience of shams, and her honest consciousness of good faith and loyalty to her duties as wife and
mother; but her incapacity for prudent intrigue was an
offence to the Court. Led by the Comte de Provence,
it sought a crime in all she did. Her use of sledges
in winter was immoral, her taste for plain white linen
instead of silk in her dress was a scheme to enrich the
Austrian Netherlands at the expense of Lyons. Her
brother's suspicious inspection of those French novelties
in manners and thought, which, as he foresaw, were to set
the world in a flame of imitation, was represented as
part of that Austrian plot, never dropped as an accusation against her whether in the gossip of Versailles or
the declamation of demagogues.

But in considering the part played by Marie Antoinette
in the tragedy of the Temple, it is unnecessary to do
more than allude to the thousand anecdotes of her
Court life, and indeed it is well to warn readers who
take their notions from memoirs of the time, that neither
those who represent the Queen as a frivolous and
extravagant devotee to amusement, or the well meaning
panegyrists who paint her without shadow, but also
without her well marked and characteristic defects, are
to be trusted, except as far as their reports are checked
by the genuine correspondence preserved at Vienna. In
it may be traced how events, and the indecisions of a
husband who had at last become attached to her and
influenced by her, obliged her to take a part in politics
for which it is no blame to her to say she was unequal.
It is impossible that even Catharine of Russia or Maria
Theresa could have averted the tempest of 1789 unless
they had found a remedy for the political weakness and
inert disposition of Louis. Marie Antoinette was possibly more powerful than they could have been in the force
of her womanhood. Had she had more, perhaps had

she had less, influence with her husband, she might have found defenders able to save the monarchy and certainly to rescue herself. The foremost powers on the demo-cratic side confessed her rightfully queen of men. Mirabeau, Lameth, Barnave; were not ashamed to be her personal subjects, swayed by her even to the reversal of their political aims. They understood the frank imperial nature which had been so misconstrued by the Lanzun's and Bezenvals, the Maurepas' and Rohans of the Court. The testimony of a man who was well acquainted with Versailles, and certainly did not sacrifice his pleasures to austerity, an associate of the Du Barrys, yet admitted to friendly companionship in the Queen's rides and daily amusements, is perhaps worth quoting as it bears on the part of the Queen's reign which has been most calumniated. The marshal Prince de Ligne writes, at the end of a charming sketch of Marie Antoinette's ordinary life, ' Her pretended flirtations were never more than a sentiment of earnest friendship for one or two persons, and a womanly and queenly coquetry which desired to please every one. Even when her youth and her want of experience might have encouraged persons to be too much at their ease in her presence, there never was one of us who had the happiness of seeing her every day, who presumed on these circumstances in the smallest particular. She acted the Queen unconsciously. We simply adored her without other thought.' Though her nobler powers were not at their best in the air of the Trianon, or of the questionable society sometimes allowed to meet her in the houses of her friends, yet her letters give abundant promise of the character afterwards de-veloped, and her observations show foresight and dis-cernment. For instance, her wish to remove the Court to Paris, her delight in the goodwill of its population while that goodwill existed, her plans for its embellish-

c

ment, some of which remain yet unfulfilled, seem to have
been political instincts that if obeyed might have averted
the march of the mob on Versailles in October, 1789.

CHAPTER IV.

Royalty in the toils.

MARIE ANTOINETTE'S chief crime in French eyes was
her wish, when all other means of preserving the
monarchy seemed hopeless, for the intervention of her
brother. But it is impossible to find even in this
disloyalty to the country she had frankly and affection-
ately adopted. Until constitutional government had
proved a sanguinary failure, she did not look abroad
for help, and even then foreign interference was desired
by her chiefly to avert the civil war and the revenges
which were threatened by the emigrant nobles on the
frontier. At the beginning of her reign, Maria Theresa
and the Austrian minister, De Mercy Argenteau, would
perhaps have had her be more Austrian than became
the Queen of France, yet her correspondence proves
her to have thrown herself only too generously into
French ideas and modes of life. Her apparent failure
in perseverance and consistency is partly excused by
the exigencies of her position as Louis XVI.'s wife.
She obviously fretted under the yoke of his indecision,
and with all her influence, which grew every year of
their lives, she could not supply him with that spark of
will without which her plans missed fire one by one.
To stand by his side, a partner in his passive endurance,
when all her being yearned for action, must have been

the worst trial endured by her. Her royal courage and spirit of self-sacrifice did not, however, fail her, and when the King well-nigh sank in discouragement, not having yet risen as he afterwards did to the height of his position, she clung more closely to him. She was in all points worthy of her post in that martyred family with which, as a family, the existing European world would do well to make itself thoroughly acquainted, recognizing in it the virtues without which no society is stable. The sufferings of the Queen were more poignant than those of its other members, and almost by her capacity for suffering may we measure the noble qualites of her nature. Her life was in more frequent danger, the insults offered to her were more vile and unceasing, and calumny fastened on her with keener cruelty than on the others. In her domestic relations she was most wounded, and it is in them that she has gained the brightest ornaments of her crown of sorrow. Her own words are the best commentary on her life, and, fortunately, so many undoubted genuine letters of hers exist that any fair mind must acknowledge her a noble, if not perfect, representative of royal womanhood.

While calumny was most busy with her name, while each day brought fresh anguish and loss, a letter from Marie Antoinette, within two months of the death of her eldest son, to Madame de Tourzel, and dated July 24, 1789, well proves that no political confusion could interfere with her minute care of her son and daughter. It was published in 1860 by Messieurs de Goncourt, and it better explains the Dauphin's character and the peculiar cruelty of his subsequent imprisonment than could any description of ours.

' My son is four years and four months old, all but two days. I do not speak of his appearance and figure, to

C 2

judge of them it is only necessary to see him. His health has always been good, but even in the cradle it was evident that his nerves were very delicate, and that the least unusual noise affected him. His first teeth were slow in coming, but they were cut without illness or trouble. It was only when cutting the last ones—I think it was the sixth—that he had a convulsion at Fontainebleau. Since then he had two others—one in the winter of 1787 or 1788, and the other when he was inoculated, but this last was very slight. From the delicacy of his nerves he is startled at any unaccustomed noise, for instance, he is afraid of dogs because he has heard them bark near him. I have never forced him to see them, because I believe that as his reason grows his fears will pass away. He is like all strong and healthy children, very thoughtless. He is quick and violent in temper, but he is good humoured, affectionate and even tender when he is not carried away by his spirits. He has a disproportionate self-love which, well guided, may some day be for his advantage. Until he is quite at his ease with any person he can control himself, and even subdue his impatience and his temper, that he may appear gentle and amiable. He keeps perfect faith when he has made a promise, but he is very indiscreet. He is fond of repeating what he has heard, and often without intending a falsehood he adds what he imagines he has seen. This is his worst fault, of which he must be thoroughly corrected. As for the rest, I may repeat that he is good humoured, and with kindness and at the same time with firmness, without being over-severe, he can be made anything of, but as he has a great deal of character for his age severity would disgust him. To give an example of it, from his earliest childhood the word "Pardon" has always revolted him. He will do and say all that is required when he is in the wrong, but the word "Pardon" is only pronounced by him with tears and the greatest difficulty. My children have always been accustomed to place great confidence in me, and when they have done wrong to tell me of it themselves, so that when I have reproved them I appeared more grieved and hurt than angry at what they had done. I have accustomed them all to consider yes or no from me as irrevocable, but I have given them for my decision a reason suited to their age, so that they should not think that I acted from caprice. My son does not know how to read, and learns very badly. He is too thoughtless to apply himself. He has no idea of haughtiness in his head, and I am most anxious that this should continue. Our children learn quite soon enough who they are.

'He loves his sister very much, and has a good heart. Whenever something gives him pleasure, whether it is to go somewhere or that he is given anything, his first impulse is to ask the same for his sister. He is naturally gay; his health requires that he should be much·in the open air, and I think that it is better to let him play and work in his garden plots on the terrace than to take him longer walks. The exercise that children take in running and playing out of doors is wholesomer than when they are forced to walk, which often tires their backs.'

The rest of the letter is a minute report of the royal children's under-governess, the Dauphin's tutor, and even of the servants attached to the school-room and nursery.

When the Queen wrote thus in 1789, and left behind her so good a proof of her motherly devotion and of her excellent sense, she was at the height of her unpopularity; her friends had fled, and left her to weep in

the inner apartments of Versailles, while the very
servants were growing insolent to her in her loneliness.
In September of the same year, there was again a stir
among the courtiers of the Œil de Bœuf. The King
hunted, made locks, dined and dozed, while plot after
plot seethed in the brains of the distracted royalists.
A plan for his removal to Metz was formed. Troops
were massed on the northern road, the Regiment of
Flanders was brought to Versailles. The banquet of the
2nd of October, was offered to them. It has been likened
to Don Juan's revelry before his summons by the
Commander. Contrary to her wishes, the Queen was
persuaded to appear at it. Followed by the King in
his hunting-dress, she entered the saloon, and holding
her son by his hand, she walked on with tears in her
eyes—radiant in beauty, and with sadness on her brow.
There was but one cry of enthusiasm when lifting the
boy in her arms she went round the tables. 'I was
delighted with Thursday,' she said afterwards. Two
days later she walked in her gardens of Trianon for
the last time. That *Via Crucis* had begun. The
intriguers and demagogues of Paris seized on the
occasion of the loyal demonstration made by the
Regiment of Flanders. 'If an insurrection is possible,'
Mirabeau had said, 'it must be one in which women
shall take the leading part.' The Insurrection of Women
followed.

But the horde of women, and men disguised as women,
which flowed forth from Paris on Versailles during the 5th
and 6th of October, were quieted by the King's reception
of them, and not till next morning did the attack on
the palace begin. Mysterious instigators to violence,
who under their costume of market-women wore silk
stockings and fashionable shoebuckles, spread through
the hungry mob. 'Monsieur, the Dauphin, and the Duke

of Orleans are alone to be spared,' was said by one of
them, as the leaders of the crowd, armed with pikes,
hatchets, and pistols, took the way of the Queen's apartments. 'We want the Queen's skin to make ribbons!'
was one of many like cries as the mob surged into
her very bed-room. One of the Gardes du Corps,
severely wounded, warned her to fly; and pale, half-
dressed, she reached the King, who had come in search
of her by a private passage. The Dauphin at the same
instant was carried in by Madame de Tourzel. For
the time the danger had passed. La Fayette and the
National Guard had arrived, and the palace was cleared.
But the insurrectionists had not forgotton their main
purpose. The King must be taken to Paris and become
the prisoner of the rabble there. He was forced to
appear at a balcony and promise that he would go.
The Queen had remained in the private apartments,
leaning, says an eye-witness, against the frame of a
window. At her right was Madame Elisabeth, and on
her left, and clinging to her, was her daughter.. Before
her, standing on a chair, was the Dauphin, who repeated
as he played with his sister's hair, 'I am hungry, mother,
I am hungry.' The Queen was told that the people
asked for her. 'Be it so,' she said. 'If it be to death,
I will go.' She took her children by their hands and
advanced. 'The Queen alone—no children!' was
unanimously shouted. Without hesitation she came
forward, her hands crossed on her breast, and the
threatening clamour ceased. One of the sudden re-
actions to which crowds gave way followed, and the
place resounded with applause and congratulation.

Soon after, by an accident, a gentleman came un-
announced on the King, the Dauphin, and the Queen,
as she was making some preparations for departure.
'We are discussing how we can lodge our good Babet,'

she said, speaking of Madame Elisabeth. 'We wish her lodged as well and as near to us as possible.' The King did not speak; then suddenly rising and taking the Dauphin in her arms she said to her husband, 'Promise me, I implore of you, promise me, for the welfare of France, for yours, for that of this dear child, that if similar circumstances recur, and that you can get away, you will not allow the occasion to escape.' The King's eyes filled with tears; without speaking he left the room.

At one o'clock, the long procession of rioters, of haggard women, some of them astride on cannon, the Paris militia, bearing on their bayonets loaves of bread, the pike-men, and the working men of St. Antoine formed themselves into a vanguard to the King's carriage. In it were the Queen, the royal family, and Madame de Tourzel. Then followed, bare-headed and captive Gardes du Corps, soldiers, and the motley multitude that had gathered to see the slow progress of Louis XVI. from Versailles to the Tuileries. At nine o'clock the royal family arrived in Paris, and were lodged in the Tuileries. The palace had been entirely unoccupied since the minority of Louis XV., and the ancient tapestries and the worm-eaten furniture had not been even put in order for the King's reception. 'Everything here is very ugly,' said the Dauphin. 'My son,' replied his mother, 'Louis XIV. was contented to lodge here.' The boy slept well, however, while Madame de Tourzel watched by his side and prepared for the anxieties of the morrow. Next day supplies of necessary furniture arrived from Versailles, and the Queen sent for her library. The Dauphin, young as he was, found less and less liberty allowed him in the garden at the Tuileries. The respectful sentries of Versailles were replaced by the citizen soldiers of La Fayette. His childish prattle was checked ; but his memory and instinctive tact were very great, and he soon learnt his untimely lesson of reticence before the spies that surrounded him.

Madame de Tourzel relates an infantine attempt at resistance that foreshadows the scenes of his revolt against Simon. 'He wished to test what he had to expect of me, and to see if I dared resist him. He refused in consequence to do something I asked of him, and said with the greatest coolness, "If you don't do what I desire I will scream ; I shall be heard from the terrace, and what will be said?" "That you are a naughty child." "But if my cries hurt me?". "I will put you to bed, and will give you a sick person's diet." On that he began to scream, to kick, and to make a fearful noise. I did not say a word to him. I had his bed made, and I asked for some broth for his supper. Whereupon he looked at me proudly, he ceased to scream, and said, "I wanted to see in what way I could take you. I see that there is nothing for me but to obey you. Forgive me, and I promise that this shall not happen again." Next day he said to the Queen, "Do you know who you have given me as my governess? She is Madame Severe!" Though he had great facility in learning what he chose, he disliked so much learning to read that he took no pains to succeed. The Queen said to him that it was shameful not to know how to read when he was four years old, and he replied, "Well, mamma, I shall know how to read as a new year's gift for you." At the end of November he said to his tutor, the Abbé d'Avaux, "I must know how long I have before New Year's Day, because I have promised mamma to know how to read by then." Finding that he had only a month left, he looked at the abbé and coolly said, "Give me, my dear abbé, two lessons a day, and I will really try and do my best." He kept his word, and went triumphantly to the Queen with a book in his hand. Throwing his arms round her neck, he said, " Here is your new year's gift. I have kept my promise and I know how to read."'

CHAPTER V.

A Prince's training.

NOTWITHSTANDING the constant alarms, and the painful circumstances of the King and Queen during their residence in the Tuileries, the education of the Dauphin went on regularly. He was taught religion, writing, history, arithmetic, geography, and botany. He was exercised in dancing and in tennis, and an attempt was made to preserve for him a corner of the Tuileries garden in which he might work and play with his pet rabbits. The same nook, enlarged and walled, was afterwards allotted to the King of Rome by Napoleon, to the Duc de Bordeaux by Charles X., and to the Comte de Paris by Louis Philippe. The Dauphin was also given the command of a regiment of boys who, falling in with the excitement of the time, had enrolled themselves in a corps and played at soldiers as seriously as did M. de La Fayette's National Guard. The curious combination of sentiment and lawlessness which existed in the first years of the revolution was well marked in a present made by his youthful regiment to their titular commandant. They brought him a box of dominoes made of the black marble that had been found in the ruins of the

Bastille. The dice were, it was said, cut out of a fragment of a mantelpiece that had belonged to the room of the Governor de Launay. Many civil speeches passed between the givers of this singular toy and the Dauphin, who had been taught to humour the fashion of the day; but he did not ask again for the dominoes, nor did the juvenile regiment long maintain its existence. 'There are no longer any children,' La Fayette had said. 'Well, since we have seen so many old men with the vices of boys, it is good to see children with the virtues of men.' The saying appears to have turned the heads of the citizen children. They imitated their elders so well that the dissolution of their corps became necessary. A few days after the King's return from Varennes, the Royal Dauphin, or, as it was scoffingly called, the Bon-bon Regiment, was reformed under the title of 'Defenders of their Country's Altar.'

Notwithstanding the Federation and its show, the new and infallible Constitution, and the quack cures tried on the sick time—perhaps by reason of them—royalty was fast losing all prestige. The little Prince had need play in his garden as unobservedly as might be, and be cautious in his words even to the poor who came with petitions to him. A woman who had some favour to ask one day said to him, 'Ah, monseigneur, if I obtained this I should be as happy as a queen.' 'As happy as a queen!' replied the Dauphin, looking sorrowfully at her. 'I know one Queen who does nothing but cry.'

He was trained to a great pity for distress by his mother, who took him to see hospitals and asylums, and even to the garrets of the poorest, and taught him to save his pocket-money for alms. He had large experience of life, for he had to play his part in the scenes

of violence and of parade that alternated round the
Tuileries.   Now presented by the Queen to the
applauding crowd in the Champ de Mars, and almost
worshipped by the excited deputies from the provinces
—now threatened and outraged on his way to St. Cloud
and on his return from Varennes, the child's nerves
must have been forced into precocious tension.   Nor
could he benefit from one great source of calm,
even to children of his age.   The free exercise of
their religion was denied to his parents as early as
the Easter of 1790.   Perplexing and injurious must
have been the spectacle of his father's enforced
worship at an altar served by an unworthy clergy
appointed by the Assembly and repudiated by Rome.

Among the various causes which decided the royal
family on their attempted flight to Montmedy, certainly
one of the most urgent was the outrage done to the
King as he was a Catholic.   When the arrangements
for escape were at last complete, on June 20, 1791,
the Queen went to the Dauphin's room, and with
some trouble awoke him.   'Get up, you are to go to
a fortified town, where you will command your regiment.'   He jumped up immediately, exclaiming, 'Quick,
quick! let us make haste; give me my sabre and my
boots, and let us go.'   He was hurriedly dressed in a
little girl's frock and cap, a disguise which had been
made for him some time before by Madame de
Tourzel's daughter.   'What is going to happen?'
asked his sister, Madame Royale.   'I think,' he
replied, 'that we are going to act a play, as we are
disguised.'   Taking her children by the hand, the
Queen led them to the place where a hackney coach
was waiting, and committed them to Madame de
Tourzel's charge.   M. de Fersen was their coach-
man, and while they waited for their parents and

Madame Elisabeth he chatted and took snuff with an inquisitive comrade who happened to be there, so as to ward off suspicion. The little Prince, disguised as Madame de Tourzel's daughter, was hidden behind her dress, and had to be still for all the long hours of unfortunate delay that passed before the King and Queen succeeded in joining the party. He bravely kept silence, even when by accident Madame Elisabeth stepped on him as she got into the carriage.

'Ah, Charles,' said his sister to him, when Postmaster Drouet had detected the King, and the revolutionary mob had gathered round the wretched family at Varennes, 'you were quite wrong, it is not a comedy.' 'I have seen it a long time,' he replied, in childish trouble and perplexity. As the hours passed in the grocer's shop at Varennes while the alarm bells rung, while royalists vainly planned desperate rescue and the swarming republicans increased in insolence and force, the children slept. The Queen showed them to the wife of the village mayor, who had taken on himself to detain the King. 'Have you no children?' she sobbed, in passionate appeal. 'You think of the King,' coolly answered the woman, 'I of my husband.'

The heat and fatigue of the return to Paris, during which the royal family suffered continual outrage from their captors and the rabble that followed them, brought on an attack of fever in the Dauphin. But no pity, no respite was given for his cure. The murder of M. de Dampierre at the carriage door because he had kissed the King's hand with respect, the shouts and revilings of the crowd, were hardly sedatives to the nervous child. When Petion and Barnave, sent by the Assembly to meet the King, got into the same carriage with the royal family, Petion,

with coarse rudeness, pulled the hair of the Dauphin
so as to make him cry. The Queen did not conceal
her vexation. 'Give me my son,' she said, for the
boy sat on Petion's knee in the crowded carriage, 'he
is used to care and to respect which have not prepared him for so much familiarity.' Barnave, whose
appearance was prepossessing, attracted the child. He
perceived on the buttons of the deputy's coat some
letters, and spelling them out he exclaimed, pleased
with his discovery, 'See, mamma, look—"Live free
or die!"' Finding the same inscription on all the
buttons, he said, 'Ah, mother, everywhere, "Live free
or die."' Barnave was deeply touched. The Queen
kept silence.

At last the procession reached Paris, in heat and
dust that were almost unendurable. In the long line
of militia that kept back the crowd the Queen looked
in vain for one kindly face. 'See, gentlemen,' she
said, 'what a state my poor children are in. They are
suffocating.' The only answer was a voice from
behind the soldiers, 'We'll suffocate you in another
manner.' When the King arrived at the Tuileries
there was a moment of extreme danger. The Queen
bravely waited in the carriage until the others had
got out. Then, almost carried by the Duc d'Aiguillon
and the Vicomte de Noailles, who were popular with
the mob, she ran for her life into the palace. Menou,
also of the revolutionary party, took the Dauphin in
his arms and preserved him for a fate worse than the
worst fury of a mob could inflict.

The circumstances of the King's journey were so
invariably unfortunate that it has been said to have
been contrived as a trap into which he should fall.
The closest watch was kept on his movements, and
the Queen could not go from her own apartment to

visit that of her son without an escort of four national guards. Even her bounties to the poor were minutely supervised. A passing relief was felt when the Assembly had at last completed the new Constitution and when the King had accepted it. This transient gleam of popularity encouraged the royal family to visit the opera and one or two public places. For a short time the expiring Assembly was pleased with the King, and even asked him for his portrait in which he should be represented showing his son the charter of the Constitution.

The Constitution contained an article providing for the education of a minor king and for that of a minor heir apparent, but it was never acted on, and as soon as the King's captivity in the Tuileries became less strict the Abbé d'Avaux resumed his charge to the great satisfaction of his little pupil. 'If I remember right,' said the abbé, 'our last lesson was on the three degrees of comparison—but have you not forgotten all about it?' 'Not at all,' replied the child; 'and to show you I have not, the positive is when I say, My abbé is a good abbé, the comparative when I say my abbé is better than another abbé, the superlative,' he continued, looking at his mother, 'is when I say my mother is the best loved and most dear of all mothers.'

The circumstances of his childhood had probably developed his intelligence, and though precocious sense is generally undesirable, it is difficult not to excuse it in the boy who had so short and troubled a span of existence, who was the heir of Charlemagne, the grandson of Maria Theresa, and who lived to be the apprentice of the Jacobin shoemaker Simon. How deeply he had been impressed by the misfortunes of his parents is shown in a dozen stories of his childish observations. One day when he came to the question

in Telemachus, one of his favourite books, 'Who is
the most unhappy of all men?' the Dauphin said,
'Let me, sir, reply to the question as if I were Telemachus. The most unhappy of men is a king who has
the pain of seeing that his people no longer obey the
laws.' On another occasion as he was playing at a
game which obliged each person to tell a story, 'I
know a funny one,' he said, when his turn came.
'There was at the door of the Assembly a crier who
sold its decrees as soon as they were printed. To
spare his words he cried, "The National Assembly for
a penny!" A passer-by joking said, "My friend, you
tell us what it is worth, but you don't tell us what it
costs."' The little Prince was, however, warned never
to speak of anything that concerned the National
Assembly.

CHAPTER VI.

Rising Tide of Revolt.

THE winter of 1791—1792 passed in continual attacks
by Jacobin intrigues on the existing Government, and
the new Constitution not having produced a golden age,
its shortcomings were chiefly attributed to the royalist
party. Nothing prospered in the troubled country, and
the cry of treachery was raised without difficulty by the
factious and ambitious members of the Opposition. The
attitude of Europe was menacing. Catharine of Russia
had taken advantage of the confusion in France to
march her troops on Poland and to threaten Constanti-
nople. It is evident from a study of the diplomacy of
the time, that Austria and Prussia did not regret sincerely

the humiliation of the French monarchy. Who among the leaders of the Mountain were in the pay of the powers that profited by the weakness of France will perhaps never be known; but the events in eastern Europe coincident with the march of revolution at Paris leave little doubt of secret understanding between some of the chiefs of the clubs and one at least of the powers that threatened the Rhine frontier.

The popular wave that overflowed the Tuileries on the 20th of June, 1792, was not so much an organized insurrection as an ebullition of the Paris rabble. It was not supported by the principal Jacobins, and was therefore perhaps all the more dangerous. But regicide had been distinctly planned, and the King had made his will two days before. The Dauphin, now seven years old, was capable of appreciating the passive courage of his father, and the heroism of his mother and aunt, while exposed to insults and to imminent danger during the occupation of their apartments by the rabble. With his mother the boy had found safety from the pressure and violence of the crowd only by placing themselves behind the table in the council-room. The Queen forced herself to put the cap of liberty on the Dauphin's head, and so flatter into forbearance the long rout that defiled before her. From early morning until ten at night the 'dangerous classes' of the faubourgs occupied the palace, and held orgies before the royal family. Pikes, muskets, and swords glittered among the rags and pale faces of the motley crowd. Some women carried naked sabres, and danced and sang the '*Ca ira.*' Torn breeches were paraded on a stick, a calf's heart inscribed 'the heart of an aristocrat,' was carried by on a pike—there was an attempt to cut down the King, whose calmness alone preserved him. Obscene words and the worst utterances of the worst women rang in the

D

children's ears, outrage appeared just verging on bloodshed when the Queen's answer to Santerre, the leader
of the mob, turned for a moment the tide of hatred.
'No one will hurt you,' he said, 'but it is dangerous to
deceive the people.' 'I am never afraid,' she replied,
'when I am with honest people.' 'How brave the
Austrian is,' was said, and for the time the danger to
her life was averted.

When night came Louis and his family, to their
inexpressible thankfulness, were again united, for during
the presence of the rioters the King had· been in a
different apartment. Deputies from the Assembly
crowded round them, half curious, half sympathetic,
and questioned them at will. A knot gathered about
the Dauphin and asked him several questions on
French history. One of them mentioned the Night
of St. Bartholomew. 'Why speak of that?' said another,
'there is here no Charles the Ninth.' 'Nor is there a
Catharine de Medici,' replied the boy. The quickness
of his answers gained for him a great success. When
next day the disturbances appeared likely to continue,
he said to his mother, 'Is it still yesterday?' Still
yesterday ; and to be still the same scene of outrage
and captivity for the three remaining years of the boy's
life !

The historian should make a particular study of the
Queen's letters during the year that preceded her final
defeat. He will so gain a true perception of her difficulties, both personal and political. We may quote here
almost at random a letter to the Empress Catharine of
Russia, which describes the situation in December,
1791, and explains those concessions of the King to the
Assembly, which had surprized and offended his brother
monarchs—

'It was necessary to agree, and so endeavour to win back the greater part of the nation, which is but misled by a horde of factious and crazy men, and also to preserve life and means of existence to the party of honest persons who still remain in France and are faithful to their King and their duty. But they are weak, and, deserted as we are, they would have been the first victims. We have not, then, been carried away by weakness. The fear of personal danger cannot affect us. The degradations we unceasingly suffer, the shameful acts we are forced to witness, powerless to stop or repress them, the vileness of all that surrounds us, the suspicion that hangs about even our most private life—is not this state a moral and continuous death, which is a thousand times worse than that which delivers from all evils?'

Yet these evils were ripening the Queen's character to its perfection. The bitterness of them is fully felt in her correspondence with her personal friends. Remembering the impetuous gaiety and frank companionship of the Trianon when the 'Comtesse Jules' was certainly neither the most prudent or grateful of friends, Marie Antoinette's last letter to her, now the emigrant Duchesse de Polignac, contains an exquisite sadness of farewell, together with full appreciation of the shadow of death and humiliation in which the royal writer walked so straight and firmly—

'Your two letters, sweet as yourself, reached me a long time since, my dearest friend. I cried over them, as I do over all your letters, and my poor broken heart sorely needed to answer you; but until now our communications have been closed, and we are so closely watched, that I fear to endanger the devoted persons

2

still in our service. But there is now a secret and sure
chance to take this letter to Turin, where it will be
posted. I use it to embrace you with all my heart
and to speak openly to you. No—do not fear poison.
It is not a fashion of this century. Calumny is used
instead. It is a surer means to kill your poor friend.
The most simple and innocent things are twisted and
envenomed, honest folk are blinded, and the mob is
intoxicated. We are described as sanguinary beings
who desire to massacre all Paris, and this when we are
prisoners and the King powerless, while, if we could,
we would purchase with our blood the welfare of France.
Good God! our enemies know this well, for they hinder
good souls among the people from coming near us. We
have, in the troubles which have overtaken us, more
need of courage than on a battlefield. Indeed, to
speak truly, it is a real one here, and if only it were
from enemies that our troubles came! Even in our
private circle few understand us. We are shackled,
and constant battles have to be fought. Better were
perpetual imprisonment in a tower by the sea than the
turmoil of constant struggle in which the weakness of
our friends and the wickedness and treachery of others
threaten us with an inevitable catastrophe. But, as you
know, I am prepared for every event. From my mother
I learned not to fear death. It comes as well to-day
as to-morrow. And so, dear heart, be very sure that
courage and strength of mind will not be wanting to
me. I only fear for my children and for those who
love me. . . . My husband gives me a thousand
messages for you and yours. The good Elisabeth
sends her love to you. She is ever an angel who helps
us to bear our griefs. She and my poor dear children
never leave me now. My daughter often speaks of
you, and your little note which was so long in reaching

us gave her infinite pleasure. Dear child, it is impossible
to be more sensitive and loving. The 'chou d'amour'
does not forget you either. He is the same as he used
to be. Farewell, dear heart. I kiss you with all my
heart. Ah! if some day! But we will not speak of
the future, it is too heartrending.

March 17, 1792.

The reader need hardly be told that the 'chou
d'amour' was the bright fair child so passionately loved
by his parents, so miserably 'got rid of' by the revolutionary powers.

Among the innumerable vexations of the Queen's life
during its later months, a large place must have been
filled by the frequent proposal and invariable ill success
of the plans made for the escape of her family. She
had the authority of Mirabeau for desiring that the
King should at any cost leave Paris, and if the flight
to Varennes was fatal to the monarchy in its event, she
was not wrong in her wish that he should escape from
the shameful bondage of the Tuileries. During the spring
of 1792, and indeed up to the eve of the 10th of August,
there were many schemes more or less plausible for
the enfranchisement of the royal family. One contrived
by Madame de Stael, and recorded in Malouet's most
valuable memoirs, may be mentioned for the glimpse
it affords of the tyranny under which the family lived.
The plan appeared singularly promising. The King,
the Queen, their children, and 'that angel who on earth
bore the name of Elisabeth,' to use the words of Lucien
Bonaparte, were to be safely taken to a house bought
by Madame de Stael on the coast of Normandy. But
it was in vain that his adherents worked for Louis; the
disease of indecision was incurable in him. He and
the Queen thanked Madame de Stael by a message, but

answered that they had reasons for not leaving Paris, and also reasons for not thinking themselves in pressing danger. Vague hopes of help from abroad, and from dealings, financial or other, with one or two chiefs of the people, were made excuses by the dilatory monarch, who indeed, not less than the Queen, was too honest to succeed in bribery or any other twilight transactions that in his extremity he attempted.

In vain Malouet wrote a letter to Louis, imploring him to leave Paris before the arrival of the Marseilles mob. It was given to the King in his wife's room, and in presence of Madame Elisabeth, Louis read it with 'emotion and inexpressible anxiety.'

'From whom is the letter?' asked the Queen.

'From Malouet. I do not show it to you because it would disturb you. He is devoted to us, but there is exaggeration in his fears and little safety in the means he proposes for our help. We shall see; nothing yet forces me to risk a dangerous game. The affair of Varennes was a lesson.'

Some hours later, about two in the morning, a gentleman of Madame Elisabeth's suite came by her orders in search of Malouet. 'The Queen and I do not know,' she said, what M. Malouet wrote to the King, but he is so uneasy, so agitated, that we wish to know what his letter contained.' Malouet sent a minute of his letter to the Princess. When she had read it she said to the messenger, 'He is right: I agree with him. I should prefer that course to all others, but we are involved in other plans. We must wait: God knows what will happen.'

'All we do is awkward and silly,' she had written some time before, yet she found herself drawn into the mistaken hope that the Jacobin leaders were less fanatic than they were corrupt. She had excellent judgment and few illusions, yet on the eve of the 10th of August she was confident that the threatened insurrection would not take place, 'Petion and Santerre having been largely bribed to prevent it.' It remains uncertain whether the money proposed was ever paid over to the two demagogues, but it is unhappily too clear that the royal family were trapped to their doom. Not in escape, but in drinking to its dregs their bitter cup, was to be their final triumph.

CHAPTER VII.

The Veto.

LOUIS had already, even before the riot of the 20th of June, accepted the end he foresaw. His thoughts dwelt persistently on the death of Charles I., and the courage and clearness of conscience never afterwards wanting in his conduct seem to have come to him with the conviction that his death at the hands of the people was politically inevitable. Warned of the results, but impassively resolved, he abruptly closed his course of conciliation and obedience to the Assembly. He refused his consent to the Girondist decrees, by which a camp of revolutionary soldiers was to be pitched at the gate of Paris, and the clergy were to be controlled and even exiled at the will of their flocks. For ten days the King sank into dejection from which it was almost impossible to rouse him. He never spoke even in his family circle, whatever efforts were made by his wife and sister to cheer him. The obstinate silence and utter self-abandonment of his son under humiliation seem to have been hereditary, and not so strangely unaccountable as some writers would assume.

There followed, on his exercise of the veto which was rightfully his by the Constitution, the storm of June, 1792, when the mob raged in and out of the royal palace at will. Whether it were indeed the mere rose-water overflow of a merry-making people or not, as has been debated, it was full of personal danger to both King and Queen, but it did not at its height of insolent menace shake the King's veto. His conscience once enlightened, he had unflinching will to obey it, and the political vacillation and the philanthropic per-plexities of the man were at last over in presence of that roused faith and piety, and consciousness of kingly right, which began to be visible in him. His dull face and heavy figure grow noble at those crises, when duty inspired him, and a greatness is now recognizable, wanting to the 'fat locksmith' of Versailles, 'who could only talk of hunting, or make school-boy jokes, or play school-boy tricks' in his hours of idleness.

Whoever else was fooled that June day, which has been called the 'day of dupes,' the King was faithful. And close and closer were drawn the family ties, as a common agony obliged the sufferers to relay those deeper foundations of human life which had been sapped at Versailles for so many generations. Seed was sown, in the tears and sweat and bloodshed of the Tuileries and the Temple, that has doubtless borne fruit, and is yet to return a large harvest of good for the use of a troubled and disorganized society. In their long passion, it is recorded how entirely and continuously the royal family forgave their persecutors. But they have done more than forgive. Never were 'the wicked' more 'like the raging sea which cannot rest, and the waves whereof cast up mire and dirt,' than since the French revolution. The family of France, standing firm on the rock of their faith, even unto death, remain as

a beacon which, it is true, lights up angry waters so that
we see their ghastly confusion, but is not the less a
steady light and warning for the use of all who read
aright the meaning of its brilliancy and judge correctly
of its indications.

As July went by, the royal family suffered daily terrors
of assassination and of separation from each other, made
worse by illusions of possible deliverance. Madame
Campan is not always trustworthy in her memoirs, but
her picture of the intimate palace life in those last
days, so distressed by apprehension and strengthened
by devotion, is evidently accurate.

'On one occasion, towards the end of July,' she writes,
'the Queen, worn out by her griefs, was sleeping,' though
a threatened riot had roused the King and Madame
Elisabeth. Louis came to know if his wife were awake,
and Madame Campan told him that she had been careful
to respect the Queen's repose. He thanked her and
said, 'I was awake and all the palace was up, the Queen
ran no risk. Oh! her sorrows are double mine.' But
when Marie Antoinette awoke and was told of what had
happened, she cried bitterly, because she had been left
to sleep. Madame Campan told her in vain that the
alarm had been groundless and that she needed to repair
her strength. 'It is not weakened,' said the Queen;
'misfortune gives great strength. Elisabeth was with
the King, and I slept. I, who would die by his side!
I am his wife, I will not have him run the slightest
risk without me.' But whatever her presentiments, the
imperial woman struggled against the destiny which no
Federation galas or Lamourette kisses of peace could
avert, and which was but hastened by her Austrian and
other kinsmen, whose inefficient brag was her worst
danger.

Madame de Stael writes of the last occasion on which

husband and wife played any part in public shows,
July 14, 1792. 'I watched at a distance the head of
the King. It was powdered, and therefore remarkable
among those which wore hair of the natural colour. His
coat, which was embroidered, was also conspicuous among
the costumes of the populace which pressed round him.
When he went up the altar steps it was as if some
victim offered itself voluntarily for sacrifice. He came
down, and crossing again the disorderly ranks of the
populace, he went and sat by the Queen and his children.
After that day the people saw him no more until he
was on the scaffold. The expression of the Queen's
face will never be effaced from my memory. Her eyes
were quite spoiled by tears. The splendour of her dress,
the dignity of her manner, contrasted with her attendants.
Only some national guards were between her and the
mob. The armed men who were assembled that day on
the Champ de Mars seemed prepared rather for a riot
than for a festival.'

The pain of doubt was nearly over. On the 26th
of July the Duke of Brunswick's manifesto drove distracted Paris to frenzy. On the 30th arrived the five
hundred fire-brands from Marseilles, all aflame with
republican fanaticism.

The visit on the 20th of June of the faubourgs to the
Tuileries had not satisfied the Jacobin leaders by its
results. Marat, from his cellar, and other more respectable
demagogues, laboured assiduously to rouse their followers
for a more serious attack on the monarchy. Petion, the
Mayor of Paris, misled by vanity, winked at the preparations openly made for an assault on the King's
palace. He believed that if Louis were dethroned he
might, as regent of a minor King, govern the country,
and he connived at the increasing turbulence of the
revolutionists. The royal family were constantly beset,

even on their private grounds, nicknamed, as has been said, 'Terre de Coblentz,' and which were separated from the terrace of the Assembly, or 'Terre de Liberté,' only by a tricoloured riband. Both the Court and the Jacobins were prepared for the struggle that must decide the fate of France ; but the feeble efforts of the despairing royalists were paralyzed by treachery and by the King's inertness. Even when the 10th of August was known to be the day chosen for insurrection, as if to encourage it no effectual measures of suppression were attempted. Five regiments and two-thirds of the Louis Guards were ordered by the Assembly to leave Paris during the last fortnight of July. The royal family had many warnings, but their doom was not to be averted. At Vespers on the Sunday before the 10th of August the musicians almost bellowed the verse, *Deposuit potentes de sede.* On the 9th none of the ladies of the household ventured to join the Queen. Alone with her sister-in-law and her children she received the only visitor who had the courage to appear—Lady Sutherland, the wife of the English Ambassador. That night the Queen and Madame Elisabeth spent in restlessly passing between their apartment and that of the King. Louis remained long with his confessor.

At twelve the alarm bells rang through Paris summoning the Jacobins to the attack. At four the day broke, and Madame Elisabeth going to a window looked out on a red angry sky and called the Queen to watch it. Presently were heard cries against the King. The Queen said nothing as she wiped away her tears. That morning she might also have heard many a scheme for her insult and destruction, and among them one that she should be paraded through the streets in an iron cage and, separated from her family, thrown into the old prison of La Force. She had not often shrunk before danger,

but she might well shudder on that day, when her brave
countenance and energetic words were worse than un-
availing to rouse goodwill in the troops who were
intrusted with the defence of the palace. 'Calumny
had already murdered her,' to use her own words, and
the few insignificant words she attempted to say were
used against her. The King's attitude was despondent.
Wig awry, with dull and heavy face clouded by care,   '
he quenched the feeble glimmers of chivalry in his
attendants.

The children meantime were dressed, and thence-
forward they did not leave their mother, who took
them with her when she went with Louis to visit the
military posts of the palace. But the King's manner
and troubled mien did not inspire confidence or loyalty,
and the Queen could scarcely check her sobs when on
her return she told an attendant, 'All is lost.' Louis
was still deliberating, when the columns of attack were
defiling from every quarter of Paris on the Carrousel.
His head was sunk in his hands when Rœderer, as
spokesman of the Directory of the Department, rushed
in and announced that the King must fly for safety
to the National Assembly. The Queen was much
excited, her eyes were heavy with crying, and 'red to
the middle of her cheeks,' reports Rœderer in his
Chronicle of fifty days. 'Never!' she exclaimed. 'Sooner
than seek shelter among our cruellest persecutors I
would have myself nailed to these walls. But are we
altogether deserted?' 'Madam, all Paris is in march;
it will be impossible to answer for the King's life—
for yours—and your children's.' 'My children!' she
said, pressing them to her breast. 'No, I will not let
them be murdered.' The King raised his head, and
after looking steadily for some seconds at Rœderer, he
turned to the Queen and said, 'Let us go also.' Only

Madame de Tourzel and the Princess de Lamballe were allowed to accompany the royal family. One of the attendants seemed resolved in his zeal to disobey the King's order to remain. The Dauphin was employed to persuade him. 'Stay here,' the child said coaxingly, 'papa and mamma order it—I implore you to stay.'

And so at seven o'clock the King and his family left the Tuileries. The Queen followed Louis, leading the Dauphin by the hand. Madame Elisabeth and her niece, the King's daughter, were next—of all the group the calmest, for even the ministers who accompanied the party were in extreme anxiety. There was great danger to them as they made their way by the furious mob on the terrace of the Assembly. The Queen was especially threatened, and a soldier in the crowd seemed continually on the point of stabbing her with a dagger which he brandished furiously. As the royal party were just entering the Assembly, he snatched the Dauphin from her side, and placed him on the desk of the secretaries. A faint cheer' broke from the deputies; but the child stretched out his arms in terror towards his mother, and the by-standers allowed him to return to her side.

CHAPTER VIII.

End of the Monarchy.

IT was decided, and the decision was curiously ironical, that the Assembly should not deliberate in the King's presence. Louis and his family were removed to a sort of cage, twelve feet square by six in height, which was used by shorthand-writers for the press. Here, crowded together, they listened to the cries and shouts of the mob as they sacked the Tuileries and massacred the Swiss Guard. The daughter of Maria Theresa must endure inertly to hear the sounds of struggle in her behalf by her adherents, and then to the sudden cessation by the King's order of their fire. Sounds of butchery and the hot steam of blood filled the narrow place in which the royal family were detained. Panting, almost suffocated, the Dauphin sat on his mother's lap, and watched her face and questioned her about the men stained with blood who brought in successively the gold and plate, the furniture and papers, that they had found in the palace. He understood the horror of the situation when a cannonier of the National Guard, not fifteen yards from the place occupied by Louis and his family, raised his bare and bloody arm with an oath before the Assembly and said, 'I offer this to you to tear out the King's heart if it be needful.' The Dauphin flung himself into his father's arms, but finding him, as ever, passive, the child, sobbing, buried his face in his mother's lap.

Successful in revolt, the Commune of Paris had during that day discovered that it was an independent power in the State. The pressure of its will forced from the hesitating Assembly a formal act, which declared the King dethroned. A new national convention — *the* Convention—was appointed to succeed the Assembly, and the Civil List was suspended. Louis was ordered to be kept a prisoner. Some silly souls, who believed that the revolution had done its worst, vainly muttered the name of Louis XVII. even within hearing of the King. Meantime, the representative of Charlemagne and Louis XIV. asked for a peach, and ate it composedly. The Queen suffered intensely. A trifling incident exemplifies the straits of the day. Her handkerchief being daubed with sweat and tears, she asked the young Count François de la Rochefoucauld, who had contrived to place himself near, for another. His own had been torn up to make a bandage for a wounded man. He went out and borrowed a napkin from the keeper of a café, but he was not allowed readmission.

The massacres continued during the night, fires were made to consume the corpses that encumbered the palace courts, and their glare helped to light the Assembly, which sat until two in the morning. Not until then was the King permitted to retire to a temporary lodging hard by in the old convent of the Feuillants. Supper was served to the royal family, but only the children could eat of it. The Queen herself carried her son from the Assembly to the cell where he was to pass the rest of the night. As they passed through the reeking insurgents, fresh from slaughter, she quieted his almost convulsive terror only by promising that he should sleep in the room she was to occupy.

The Queen's spirits rose, as some think unaccountably, during the three days that were spent between the

A

reporters' box at the Assembly and the cells of the Feuillants. She and the King had till now been face to face with a pseudo but pretentious Constitution and Parliament, but after the 10th of August the Commune had revealed itself as a tyranny, fierce, unreasoning, almost childish in its sudden impulses, but all the more terrible in its irresponsibility. All illusion was at last over, and henceforth the courage of Louis and his wife rose before their inevitable fate to the level of its cruelties. The Queen, after the exhaustion of the first shock, could smile, as she did, to hear the orders given for petty insults to royalty ; and the King's calm was unmoved when desired to observe that the shattered statues of his predecessors were examples of how kings should be used by the people. 'It is fortunate,' he quietly remarked, 'that its fury should only wreak itself on inanimate objects.'

On Monday, August 13, the royal family, the Princess de Lamballe, and some members of their household were removed to the Temple, but none of their servants were allowed to accompany them except those appointed by Petion and the Commune.

The mob vied with the authorities in affronts to the King as he was slowly conducted to the prison appointed for him. The Queen was advised by Petion to look on the ground lest the people should think her proud and assault her. Two hours of reviling and outrage were endured by the hapless group, and it was seven o'clock when the royal family arrived in the court of the old citadel of the Templars. At first they were served with supper in the part of the vast building which was called the palace, but afterwards an officer of the Commune, lantern in hand, showed the King the room which he was now to occupy. It was lighted only by a single window. Louis entered calmly ; he took down from the walls some indecent prints, and prepared himself for peaceful sleep. The royal family were without plate, linen, or even a change of clothes; but no privation could affect them seriously, while the events of the 10th of August were yet recent. 'Did I not say so?' was the Queen's only word to Madame de Tourzel as she leant over the tired Dauphin's bed. Then she resumed the patient courage which remained with her to the end, and busied herself in arranging the rooms which her husband and children were to occupy.

The Temple tower was even then gloomy with memories of the disgraced Templars, but the execution by fire of Jaques Molay and Guy of Auvergne is forgotten now in the newer interest of the great Bourbon tragedy. The King and his family had not been a week in the austere fortress when they were deprived of their attendants. Mesdames de Lamballe and de Tourzel and the rest of the scanty suite were sent to the prison of La Force, and only M. Hue, who had been about the Dauphin's person, was readmitted to the King's service. The arrangement of the three apartments allotted to the royal family, and which occupied the three stories of the tower, were necessarily altered. The Dauphin's bed was placed in his mother's room; Madame Elisabeth and Madame Royale took his empty lodging.

The days, so full of turmoil without, passed tranquilly for the dethroned family. The King's irresolutions were at last over, and he appears to better advantage as the simple father and husband than when he was called on to act as beseemed a monarch. He got up between six and seven, shaved and dressed himself, and then shut himself into the closet in the turret off his room, where he recited his prayers and read until breakfast. 'His piety,' writes M. Louis Blanc, 'seemed to have acquired, since his dethronement, a particular stamp of resignation,

E

and if it happened that he was inconvenienced in the
discharge of his religious duties, he showed neither
irritability or resentment. On Friday, whether from forgetfulness or ill will, the officials who waited on his table
having only served meat, he sopped a bit of bread in a
glass of wine and said, with a smile in which there was
no bitterness, "There is my dinner."' He was at all times
watched, for it was the duty of the municipal officer on
service to keep him always in sight. The Queen rose
earlier than her husband, and she dressed her son and
heard him say his prayers. She then admitted M. Hue
to clean her room, and with him came municipals, whose
duty it was to pass the day in her apartment, though at
night they slept in the ante-room which separated her
room from that of Madame Elisabeth. At nine the
princesses and the Dauphin went to breakfast with the
King, after which Louis taught his boy French, Latin,
history, and geography. Marie Antoinette occupied herself with her daughter, to whom also Madame Elisabeth
gave lessons in drawing and arithmetic. At one o'clock,
if the weather were fine, and if Santerre, the chief of the
National Guard, happened to be present, the family
walked during an hour in the garden, principally for the
Dauphin's health. Dinner was at two o'clock in the
King's room; afterwards the children played awhile in
the Queen's apartment. The King sometimes dozed,
while the princesses worked. Towards evening the
family gathered round the table, and the Queen or
Madame Elisabeth read aloud from some work suited
to the entertainment and instruction of the young
people. We hear of Miss Burney's *Cecilia* among the
favourite books. At eight M. Hue served the Dauphin's
supper in Madame Elisabeth's room. His parents looked
on, and the King proposed a riddle or two out of a collection which he had found in some old newspapers on

the bookshelves. After supper, the little Prince undressed himself and said his prayers, which included
one for Madame de Lamballe and one for Madame de
Tourzel. When the municipals on service were near,
the child had sufficient discernment to say them in a
low voice. Then the King, silently pressing his wife's
hand, retired to his turret and stayed there, in silent
communication with his God, until midnight, when he
went to bed.

The princesses generally sat up awhile, working at the
clothes that required mending. Sometimes they waited
until the King had undressed that they might patch the
only coat he had brought to the Temple. The Dauphin
was better supplied, for Lady Sutherland had sent for his
use, on the night of the 10th of August, some clothes
belonging to her son, who was of the same age.

The King occupied himself assiduously in training the
Dauphin, who began to repay largely the care spent on
him. With exquisite feeling, the child, now seven and
a half years old, accommodated himself to every privation. He never spoke of Versailles and the Tuileries,
and did not seem even to remember his toys and games
in those happier times. He already knew by heart the
best of La Fontaine's fables and passages from Corneille
and Racine. His writing was excellent, and in dictation
he hardly made any mistakes of spelling. He was at
home even in the new geography of Departmental France.
The Queen was equally devoted to her daughter, and
educated her in all womanly and Christian virtue.
'My children,' said the King one day, 'the summary
of life is love, labour, and prayer.' He had well described the life of his family in the Temple.

And while the system of Jacobin propagandism was
invented, which led at last to the expenditure, in one
year, of twenty-four millions sterling on the fifty thousand

Revolutionary Committees of France, the King had not
£20 at his disposal. To pay for the commonest necessaries he was forced to borrow from his valet. It is but
fair to say that at first the personal needs of the King
were liberally supplied by the Commune. A very
abundant table was supplied, chiefly however for the
benefit of the officials on duty, as the royal family
remained austerely abstemious. It is probable that the
insolence and cruelty of the officials was more personal
than officially ordered, yet instances of petty tyranny,
almost incredibly absurd, were daily multiplied. For
example, the study of arithmetic was forbidden to the
Dauphin, lest he might use figures for secret correspondence. On the 2nd of September, Hue was arrested
and brought before the new tribunal of the Commune,
and he reappeared no more at the Temple. He was
accused of having introduced a box of tricoloured
ribbons into the King's prison, of having ordered a pair
of breeches of 'Savoyard colour,' which implied a
private intelligence with the King of Sardinia, and
other similar offences. The massacres of September
were going on during his trial, and he was only spared
instant execution in the hope that he might betray some
secret of his master. After extraordinary peril he was
released, and lived to render what service he could to
the royal family, though he was not again admitted to
the Temple. He saw the restoration of the Bourbons
in 1815, and published an interesting narrative of what
he had himself witnessed of the sufferings of Louis and
his family. Clery, who had formerly belonged to the
household, replaced him in the Temple. At first the
prisoners distrusted the new-comer; but he soon gained
their confidence, and repaid it by his fidelity to the end.

There is no occasion here to describe the massacres
of September, except so far as they actually touched the

royal family and contributed to the Dauphin's terror and
to the almost unbrightened gloom of his young life.
The panic which led to them, and which was skilfully
fomented by the Jacobin chiefs, is sufficiently explained
by the circular sent by Danton, then Minister of Justice,
to the towns of France, while the massacres were still
going on in Paris. On the 3rd of September he dictated
—for Danton never wrote himself—the message that is,
perhaps, the worst blot on his name. 'The Paris
Commune hasten to inform their brethren in all the
Departments that the people have put to death a part
of the ferocious conspirators detained in the prisons.
This act of justice appeared indispensable, in order
that, at a moment when the nation was about to march
towards the enemy, the legions of traitors within the
walls might be restrained. No doubt the entire nation,
after the long course of treachery which has brought her
to the edge of the abyss, will at once adopt this measure,
which is so necessary for the public welfare ; and all
Frenchmen will exclaim like the men· of Paris, "We
march to meet the enemy, but we will not leave brigands
behind us to massacre our wives and children." '

This official approval of crime by the Minister of
Justice, enables us to realize the condition of Paris
and the peril of the Temple prisoners during the three
days of bloodshed. Except however from the hurry
and mysterious manner of their gaolers, they did not
know, during the first days, what was passing without.
The death of Madame de Lamballe seems first to
have turned the violence of the 'Septembriseurs' in
the direction of the Temple. We may hope that
Marie Antoinette never knew the atrocities committed
that mid-day in the street, where her dearest friend
was cut to pieces : atrocities not surpassed by any
of which we have heard during the Indian Mutiny.

Madame de Lamballe's heart and other fragments of
her body were carried on pikes to the gate of the '
Temple. Before a barber's shop, her head was washed,
and her hair was dressed after the fashion of the day. .
Wine was got from a tavern and poured through the
bloodless lips, and as it trickled below, a drummer,
Charlat, drank the polluted drops. The same man
afterwards, with a companion, cooked and ate the heart
of the noble and faithful lady.

When the rabble arrived at the Temple there seemed
no hope but that the Queen, if not her sister and her
children, would share Madame de Lamballe's fate.
Knowing that resistance would be useless, the municipal officer on service threw the gates open, but hung
across them a tricolour riband, from behind which he
harangued the reeking murderers. They have been
praised for respecting the emblem of the republic, but
the incident proves rather the untrustworthiness of
'public opinion'—for what temper is that which will
sanction crimes too horrible for narration, and within
the same hour pay theatrical reverence to a popular
colour? The severest criticism on public opinion would
be a history of its vagaries, and one of the strangest
of these was surely this halt of cannibals before the
riband that guarded the Temple.

Four deputies from the mob were admitted to see
the King. They insisted that the royal family should
appear at the window. One of the officers of the day
tried to keep back the King, but the leader of the
deputation exclaimed, 'They want to hide from you
Lamballe's head, which has been brought here, to
show you how the people revenge themselves on
their tyrants. I advise you to appear if you do not
wish them to come up.' The Queen fell fainting to
the ground, and was carried to an inner chamber

where the cries and insults of the rabble were less audible. For six hours it was still uncertain whether the royal family would not be massacred, but towards night the mob drew off to continue their work in the prisons, where, according to the lowest estimate of a Jacobin writer, fourteen hundred and eighty souls perished.

'The tumult was hardly over,' writes Madame Royale, ' when Petion, instead of busying himself to stop the massacre, coolly sent his secretary to my father to count out some money.' It was an advance of £80—paid however in assignats—on the sum nominally allowed for the King's expenses; and it was sorely wanted, for the children were without even a sheet of paper for their lessons, and the Queen was troubled about the price of a watch she had ordered from Breguet, and for which she had not been able to pay. Among the little luxuries ordered by the King were some toys for the Dauphin, for which he had longed with all the anxiety of a prisoner. But he could have had few opportunities of playing with them. The officers of the Commune grew more and more insolent in their surveillance, and the family met each day with some new insult. The walls that they had to pass when they went out for their daily exercise were scribbled over with threatening inscriptions, such as, 'Madame Veto shall trip it,' 'We shall know how to keep the big pig in order,' 'Down with the Austrian she-wolf,' 'The wolf cubs must be strangled.' Figures of the King hanging on a gallows were drawn, with the inscription, 'Louis taking an air bath,' or a guillotine with the words, 'Louis spitting in the sack.' Not all the attendants, however, were cruel, and some rare kindly looks and words cheered the captives from time to time.

On the 21st of September, the National Convention met for the first time. It had been chosen by a minority of the people, under the influence of violence and panic, to do the will of the Jacobin Club and the Paris Commune. Its first act was to proclaim the republic, and from their windows the royal family could hear the crier announcing their own deposition. Not long after, the affair of the iron safe discovered at the Tuileries, and which contained some papers of the King's, was used by Roland the Girondin, and of course by other revolutionary leaders, to whet the minds of the public, and to create fresh 'public opinion' in the direction of the trial of Louis. The little Prince heard some rumour of the business, and one day he raised almost a ferment in the Temple by saying at dinner when a cake was served of which he was fond, 'Mamma, there is a good cake. If you like I will put it in the cupboard here and it will be safe. No one, I assure you, will be able to get at it.' Every eye glanced round to discover the mysterious hiding-place. The municipals grimly mused over a fresh denunciation—when the Queen said, 'My son, I do not see the cupboard of which you speak.' 'Here it is, mother,' he replied, pointing to his mouth. It was a curious gleam of childish satire on the trifling charges brought against his father.

CHAPTER IX.

Prison.

On the 29th of September, the royal family were removed to their apartments in the principal tower, which abutted on the smaller keep which had been their temporary lodging. It was decreed that the Dauphin should be removed from the care of his mother, and remain entirely with the King except at meal-times, the only hours when, by a new regulation, the family were allowed to meet. The boy was indignant at the cruelty of the order. 'Dost thou know,' said an official to him, 'that liberty has made us all free, and that we are all equal?' 'Equal as much as you please,' retorted the Dauphin, 'but it is not here,' he added, looking at his father, 'that you will make me believe that liberty has made us free.' The greater tower of the Temple, which had been roughly prepared for the royal family, was a square gloomy pile of some hundred and fifty feet in height, with an interior of from thirty to thirty-six feet either way. It had been used as a treasure-house by the Templars, and in it, after their suppression in 1307, Philippe le Bel had established his court. The walls were nine feet thick, which must have made the chambers within extraordinarily gloomy. There were four floors, to which the only access was by a staircase that wound up one of the four turrets at the angles. The ground floor was used by the municipal officers not actually on service in the royal apartments, and was called the council-room. The guard on duty occupied the first floor, in the second were lodged the King, the Dauphin, and their servant Clery. ' The third was used by the Queen and the princesses. The fourth was empty. In the ante-chamber to the King's bed-room was hung up the ' Declaration of the rights of man.' On the tiles of the fireplace were inscribed ' Liberty, Equality, Property, Security.' The clock on the mantelpiece was by ' Lepanti, clockmaker to the King,' but a wafer had been stuck over the word ' King.' Simple and scanty furniture, but still sufficiently comfortable, had been provided for the use of the prisoners. Eight officers of the Commune, of whom one was always with the King, and one with the Queen, were chosen by lot for daily service. The outer guard of the whole inclosure of the Temple was kept by a force of two hundred and eighty-seven men until after the King's execution, when it was reduced to two hundred and eight.

The habits of the family in their new lodging remained much the same as before. On rising, Louis read the office of the Order of Knights of the Holy Spirit. A Mass in the prison had been refused even on days of obligation, and he had bought a Paris Breviary for his own use. Four hours he daily gave to the Latin authors, and he also read many books of travel, Montesquieu, Buffon, Hume's *History of England*, Tasso, in Italian, and most of all and constantly, the *Imitation of Jesus Christ*, in Latin. It is said that during the five months of his captivity he read two hundred and fifty-seven volumes.

' It is conceivable,' writes M. Louis Blanc, ' that this manner of life was calculated to touch hearts in

which a spark of feeling remained. The private virtues
of Louis XVI., the unchanging sweetness of Madame
Elisabeth, the ingenuous charm of the captive child,
and the Queen's dignity—a dignity entirely noble
now that it was softened by misfortune, were brought
into strong relief and under the observation of the
municipal officers on duty. When, holding in his
hand the roll of 'bread just brought to him, Louis
offered half to Clery, and observed, "It seems that
your breakfast has been forgotten; take this, the rest
is enough for me," or when the haughty daughter of
Maria Theresa made her own bed without a murmur.
Every republican heart must surely have been touched.'

The Queen, however brave, was not equally passive.
The daughter of the Cæsars fretted against her prison
bars in keenest suffering, yet she was ever unselfish
and noble in her long anguish, and patient in the
presence of insult and suspicion. Probably her chief
earthly consolation was in the childish devotion of her
son, who, with the fine tact that had always distinguished him, tried to cheer her with any scrap of
good news that might affect them. He used to run
to her and tell her if any municipal arrived who was
less insolent than the others, and repeat to her any
expression of good feeling among the guards and
attendants.

The hour at last drew on for the trial of the King.
The Constituent Assembly had weakened royalty, the
Legislative Assembly had left Louis a prisoner, the
Convention being, like the others, an agent of 'progress,'
had no other choice but to decree his death. Jacobin
and Girondin alike, bidding not merely for power but
for life from the Paris mob, must needs vote the
King's execution. The current they had let loose was
sweeping liberal men from every standing-point. The

mockery of the King's trial was a consequence of his first concessions to violence.

Towards the end of October, the preparations for it were begun. There were not wanting brave hearts eager to affront the danger of pleading for him at the bar of the Assembly. A lieutenant-colonel and a young girl were equally ready. From Germany, Schiller sent an elaborate defence, and Sheridan spoke of coming himself to France to undertake the case. It was finally intrusted to Tronchet, the venerable Malesherbes and De Sèze, but the King foresaw that their efforts in his behalf would be useless.

When Louis was summoned before the Convention on the 11th of December, the Queen's proud reserve before her gaolers broke down for the first time. The Dauphin was brought to her at eleven o'clock, and at one the Mayor of Paris and other officials came for the King. Uncertain of his fate, Marie Antoinette besought the municipal on service in her room to inform her of what was going on, but he gave her no satisfaction. On the return of Louis from the Convention, where his patient bearing had impressed even Marat with astonishment and compassion, he was finally separated from his family except for their one last interview. 'From my son! my son who is only seven years old!' he exclaimed in bitter grief, when he was told that he should be kept apart from his wife and children. The Queen gave up her bed to the Dauphin and sat beside it in such silent agony of sorrow, that her sister and daughter dared not leave her. A note, pricked with a pin on paper by Madame Elisabeth and slipped into the King's napkin by one of the attendants, reached its destination. Louis replied by one concealed in a ball of thread, and after a time a communication between the King's and Queen's apartments was contrived by means of a string, which let down notes from the floor above to the window of the turret chamber, to which Louis was allowed to retire for prayer. An hour for their transmission was agreed upon; when it arrived, Clery, on some trifling pretext, closed the door and kept the municipal present in conversation, while the King received and returned the precious messages of love and duty.

On Christmas Day the will of Louis XVI. was written. It remains a noble witness to his thoughts at such a time; of it Madame de Stael writes, 'Every word was a virtue.' Yet so extraordinary was the abberration of men's minds that it was printed by the Commune as a testimony to the fanaticism and crimes of the King. Often reprinted as it has been, it yet affords such fair measure of the strength and faith and charity which were found in the naturally dull and shy man when tested in the furnace of his trial, that it is well to give it to readers especially interested in his private life and ideas.

'In the name of the Holy Trinity, of the Father, the Son, and the Holy Ghost. To-day, the twenty-fifth day of December, 1792, I, Louis, the sixteenth of that name, King of France, having been more than four months shut up with my family in the tower of the Temple at Paris, by those who were my subjects, and deprived of all communication whatsoever since the 11th instant with my family; moreover, being implicated in a trial of which, seeing the passions of men, it is impossible to foresee the issue, and for which no means or pretext are to be found in any existing law, having God alone as witness to my thoughts, and to whom I may address myself, I declare here in His presence my last will and my sentiments.

'I leave my soul to God my Creator. I beg Him to receive it in His mercy, and not to judge it according to its merits, but by those of our Lord Jesus Christ, who offered Himself in sacrifice to God His Father for us men, however unworthy, and for me most so of all.

'I die in the communion of our holy mother the Catholic Apostolic and Roman Church, which holds its powers by an uninterrupted succession from St. Peter, to whom Jesus Christ intrusted them. I never presumed to be judge in the different modes of dogmatic explanation which rend the Church of Jesus Christ, but I have always accepted and shall ever accept, if God give me life, the decisions which ecclesiastical teachers united to the Holy Catholic Church give and shall give in conformity to the discipline of the Church followed since Jesus Christ. I pity with all my heart our brothers who may be in error, but I do not pretend to judge them, and I not the less love them in Jesus Christ, according to the dictates of Christian charity.

'I pray God to forgive me all my sins. I have sought scrupulously to know them, to detest them, and to humble myself in His presence. Not being able to obtain the ministry of a Catholic priest, I pray God to receive the confession which I have made of them, and above all to accept my profound repentance for having put my name (though it was against my will) to deeds which may be contrary to the discipline and faith of the Catholic Church, to which I have always remained heartily and firmly united. I pray God to accept my firm resolve, if He accord me life, to seek the ministry of a Catholic priest, as soon as I can, to make confession of all my sins and to receive the Sacrament of Penance.

'I beg all whom I may have inadvertently offended (for I do not remember having knowingly offended any one), or those to whom I may have given scandal or bad example, to forgive me whatever wrong they think I may have done them. I beg all who are charitable to unite their prayers with mine to obtain from God the forgiveness of my sins. I forgive with all my heart those who have been my enemies without my having given them cause, and I pray God to forgive them, as also those who by false or mistaken zeal have wrought me much evil.

'I recommend to God, my wife, my children, my sister, my aunts, my brothers, and all those who are attached to me by ties of blood or by other bonds whatsoever. I pray God specially to cast His merciful eyes on my wife, my children, and my sister, who have suffered so long with me, to sustain them by His grace if they should lose me, and for as long as they remain in this perishable world.

'I recommend my children to my wife. I have never doubted of her natural love for them. I particularly recommend to her to make of them good Christians and honourable persons, to make them esteem the greatness of this world (should it be their fate to know it) as but a dangerous and perishable good, and to turn their eyes towards the one true and lasting glory which is eternal. I beg my sister to continue her kindness to my children, and to be to them a parent if they should unhappily lose their mother.

'I beg my wife to forgive me all the evils she suffers for my sake, and the vexations I may have caused her in the course of our union, as she may be sure that I remember nothing on her part, should she think herself in any way to blame. I very strongly desire my children, after their duty to God, who is before all, to remain always submissive, united, and obedient to their mother, and grateful for all the care and trouble she takes for them, and in memory of me I beg them to consider my sister as a second mother.

'I desire my son, if he have the misfortune to become King, to remember that he is to devote himself entirely to the good of his fellow-citizens, and that he ought to forget all hatred and all resentments, and especially such as relate to the misfortunes and wrongs which I suffer: that he can only give welfare to his people by reigning according to law, but at the same time that a King can only insure respect for law and do the good which is in his heart, in proportion as he possesses the necessary authority, and that otherwise being tied in his actions and inspiring no respect, he is more mischievous than useful.

'I desire my son to take care of all the persons who were attached to me, as far as the circumstances in which he will be placed will permit; to remember that the debt is sacred which I have contracted towards the children or relations of those who have perished for me, as well as towards those who have been unfortunate because of me. I know that many persons who had been attached to me have not behaved towards me as they should, and have even shown ingratitude to me, but I forgive them (in moments of disturbance and effervescence men are not masters of themselves), and I beg my son, if he find occasion, to think only of their misfortune.

'I wish I could here express my gratitude to those who have shown me a true and disinterested attachment. On the one hand, if I were sensibly affected by the ingratitude and disloyalty of men to whom, as well as to their relations and friends, I have never shown aught but kindness, on the other side I have had the consolation of witnessing the gratuitous interest and attachment that many persons have shown me; I beg them to receive my best thanks. In the present condition of affairs, I should fear to compromise them were I to speak more plainly, but I specially desire my son to seek occasion of recognizing such persons.

'I should, however, believe myself unjust to the feeling of the nation if I did not openly recommend to my son Messieurs de Chamilly and Hue, whose true attachment to me induced them to imprison themselves with me in this sad place, and who have been well nigh victims to their devotion. I also recommend to him Clery. I have but to speak in praise of his attentions since he has been with me. As it is he who now remains with me to the end, I beg the gentlemen of the Commune to give him my personal effects, my books, my watch, and the other trifles which have been deposited with the Council of the Commune.

'I forgive very willingly the ill-treatment and annoyances which those who guarded me have thought fit to practise towards me. I have met kindly and pitiful souls among them. May they be blessed at heart with that peace which they have earned by their charitable thoughts.

'I beg MM. de Malesherbes, Tronchet, and Sèze to receive here my best thanks, and the expression of my sense of the care and trouble they undertook for me. I end by declaring before God, and ready to appear before Him, that I do not reproach myself with any of the crimes laid to my charge.

'Done in duplicate, in the tower of the Temple, the 25th of December, 1792.

'LOUIS.'

CHAPTER X.

Preparation for Death.

IN a conversation with his friends and legal defenders, which has been recorded, the King summed up the characters and lives of his wife and sister in a few sentences, which throw valuable light on the family, as it was even in those days when the Queen's thoughtlessness and wilfulness left room for the misconstructions of a venomous Court. Louis had been for a day or two uneasy about his daughter's health. By private communications from the room overhead he knew that she was ill. His fatherly anxiety turned his thoughts from politics, and he spoke freely of his domestic life. ' In the midst of all my misery,' he said, ' Providence allowed me consolation: my life has been sweetened by my children, by my Queen, and by my sister. I will not speak of my children, already so unhappy, even at their age !' he added with emotion, 'nor of my sister, whose life has been one of devotion, affection and courage. Spain and Piedmont appeared to wish for her alliance at the death of Christine de Saxe ; the canonesses of Remiremont offered to elect her abbess, but nothing could separate her from me. She attached herself to my misfortune as others had attached themselves to my prosperity. But I wish to speak to you of a subject which causes me great pain : the injustice of the French to their Queen. If they knew her true worth, if they knew the degree of perfection to which, since our troubles, she has risen, they would revere and cherish

her, but for long her enemies and mine have had the art
of sowing calumnies among the people so as to change
into hatred the love of which she was once the object.'

'You saw her,' he continued, 'arrive at Court. She
was little more than a child. My grandmother and my
mother were no more : my aunts were there, but they
had not the same title to influence her. Placed in the
centre of a brilliant Court, in presence of a woman who
lived and was supported by intrigue, the Queen, then
Dauphiness, had before her eyes a daily example of
extravagance and splendid show. What opinion must
she not have gathered of her own power and rights—
she who was the rightful heir and owner of such a
position ? To live in the society of Madame du Barry
was unworthy of the Dauphiness. Obliged to adopt
a sort of retirement, she made for herself a life free
from restraint. On the throne she continued the habits
so acquired. These manners, which were new to the
Court, were too much in accordance with my own tastes
for me to desire to check them. I did not then
know how dangerous it was for sovereigns to admit
too close an intercourse with their subjects. Familiarity
saps the respect which should surround those who
govern. At first the public applauded the abandonment of ancient customs, of which afterwards they made
a crime.

'The Queen wished to have friends. The Princesse
de Lamballe was the one most distinguished by her.
Her conduct in our subsequent misfortunes amply
justified the Queen's choice. The Comtesse Jules de
Polignac pleased her. She made her her friend. At
the request of the Queen I bestowed on the Comtesse,
afterwards Duchesse de Polignac, kindnesses which
begat envy in others. The Queen and her friend were
subjected to the most unjust animadversion.

F 2

'Even her regard for her brother, the Emperor Joseph II., was attacked by calumny. It was first insinuated, then printed in several newspapers, and finally affirmed in the tribune of the National Assembly, that the Queen sent many millions to Vienna for the Emperor ; an atrocious calumny which was triumphantly refuted by a deputy.

'Factious men have thus passionately vilified and blackened the Queen that they may better prepare the people for the end. Yes, my friends ; her death is determined. If her life were spared they fear she might avenge me. Unfortunate Princess ! Her marriage promised her a crown, but to-day what a future is before her !' The King's eyes filled with tears as he spoke, and his hand listlessly fell on the hand of M. de Malesherbes.

The story of the midnight vote by which 'Death' was decided has been often told. The scene of panic, turbulence, passion and falsehood, attended by the painted and mincing fine ladies in the gallery, just as any other drama might be, is in strong contrast with the calm but terrible suffering of the family in the Temple during the brief space left to the King. Twenty-four hours only were allowed to him after the notification of his sentence.

In every one of the numerous histories of the French Revolution the trial of the King may be read with the same detail of well known incident. The form of his indictment summed up the suspicions of the people as they had been fostered by the revolutionary party. 'Yet, as must be confessed,' writes M. Louis Blanc, 'of the actions for which he was arraigned some were sought to be established by implication, rather than by proof, and much that seemed treachery to the nation had been absolutely forced by circumstances on the

King.' Of course the ready accusation of equivoca-
tion in reply to his cross-examination was brought
against Louis. He was careful to spare his friends,
and he was certainly confused in one or two answers
to questions in which traps were laid for him, yet,
when all is said by his enemies, must not his defence
by De Sèze be fully accepted? It concludes with a terse
and vigorous statement of the King's career.

'Louis came to the throne at twenty, and at twenty
he on the throne set an example of moral goodness.
He brought it to no unworthy weakness or corrupting
passion. He was frugal, just and severe. He showed
himself ever the constant friend of the people. The
people wished for the removal of a tax which pressed
on them. He removed it. The people demanded the
abolition of servitude. He abolished it first in his own
domains. The people desired reforms in criminal legis-
lation, by which those accused should be less severely
treated. He made those reforms. The people desired
that the thousands of Frenchmen who by the rigour of
our customs had been deprived of rights that belong
to citizens should acquire or recover those rights. He
by his laws restored them. The people desired liberty.
He gave it. He even by personal sacrifices anticipated
their wishes, and yet in the name of that people it is
to-day demanded—— Citizens, I will not conclude.
I pause in the presence of history. Remember that
before it will your judgment be arraigned, and that
centuries will endorse the final award."

From M. de Malesherbes' account of the King's last
days it is known that Louis suppressed the pathetic
peroration which had been prepared by M. de Sèze.
'It must be omitted,' he said ; 'I will not seek to
excite their pity.' Words in which De Maistre recognized not pride, but the will to suffer and the instinct

of expiation, which makes of the King's death a sacrifice.

The serene calm of his attitude, conscious of duty, using all lawful means of appeal from the injustice of his trial, yet more in the interests of others than his own, was worthy of his position.

M. de Malesherbes, whose duty it was to inform the King that sentence of death had been passed on him, found him sitting, his back towards the door, and resting his face on his hands. The noise made by his counsel in coming in roused him from his meditation. He got up to receive them and said, 'For two hours I have been searching my memory if during my reign I have intentionally given my subjects just cause of complaint against me. Well! I swear to you in all the sincerity of my heart, as a man about to appear before God, I have always willed the good of my people, and I never had a wish to oppose it.'

The King listened attentively to the details of the vote which had decreed his death. He deprecated any further attempt to save his life, and forbade all armed interference ; but, by the urgent advice of his defenders, he signed the following paper—

'I owe it to my honour and to my family not to admit a judgment which finds me guilty of a crime with which I cannot reproach myself. In consequence I appeal to the nation itself from the judgment of its representatives, and by these presents I give my defenders special powers and I lay as a charge on their fidelity to make known, by all the means at their disposal, this appeal to the National Convention, and to request that it be mentioned in the report of its sittings.

'Done in the tower of the Temple, January 16th, 1793.

'LOUIS.'

'It is rather in the interest of the people than in that of the King that we have asked for this declaration,' observed De Sèze. 'No,' replied the King, with a kindly smile impossible to describe, 'you ask it much more in my interest than in that of the people, but I give it to you much more in its interest than in my own. The sacrifice of my life is a small thing compared to the glory and the welfare of the people, and do not think, gentlemen, that the Queen and my sister will show less strength and resignation than I shall. Death is preferable to their fate.'

The King on more than one occasion spoke with clear foresight of the coming anarchy and bloodshed which would desolate his people. He showed a judgment and intellect which had been obscured hitherto by his reserve and shyness. During his captivity he read at all spare hours, and on the 18th of January he was chiefly occupied with the volume of English history which relates the death of Charles I. His counsel were not allowed to see him after his condemnation. Perquisitions were made in his room as if he were already dead. He was watched night and day, minute precautions were taken to remove every cutting instrument, and even a fork to eat with was refused him. At two o'clock on the 20th of January he was officially informed of the decree which condemned him to death. His attitude was one of singular dignity as the fifteen or sixteen persons who were deputed by the Commune and the Convention entered his room. When the paper had been read in a trembling voice by the secretary of the Council, notifying that in twenty-four hours the decrees of the Convention would be executed, Louis took it, and folding it, placed it quietly in his pocket-book, from which he at the same time took a letter which he desired might be given to the Convention. The Minister of

Justice, to whom the King handed it, hesitated, but Louis begged to read aloud his few last requests touching a confessor and the future of his family and servants.

The vilest as the noblest of his subjects appear to have felt that the King's death had other meanings than the obvious murder of an innocent man. Marat, who had dressed himself to hear Louis arraigned in a new suit of clothes as on a festival, yet could not refrain from writing in his paper the day after the King had appeared at the bar of the Convention—'If innocent, how great he would have seemed to me in his humiliation.'

Chaumette, in whose charge was the Temple and its prisoners, became ill under the strain of his work. Hébert, the infamous editor of 'Père Duchesne,' has left this singular record of his feelings. He writes— 'I wished to be of the number of those who were to be present when the sentence of death was read to Louis. He listened to it with rare coolness. When it was finished he asked for his family, a confessor, in short whatever could help him in the last hour. He showed such dignity, nobleness, and greatness in his manner and words that I could not bear it. Tears of rage rose to my eyes. There was in his looks and demeanour something visibly supernatural to man. I left the room wishing to check my tears which flowed in spite of me, and fully resolved to have done with my office. I opened my heart to one of my colleagues who was no more able to go on than I was, and I said to him in my usual plain speech—"My friend, the priests who are members of the Convention, and who, notwithstanding their sacred office, voted for death, made the majority which delivers us from the tyrant. Let these constitutional priests accompany him to the scaffold. Only constitutional priests are cruel enough to fill such an office."'

And so it came about that the two municipal priests, Jacques Roux and Jacques Claude Bernard, were chosen to conduct Louis to his death. Bernard was guillotined with Robespierre on the 10th Thermidor; Roux avoided public execution by suicide.

The Abbé Edgeworth de Firmont who had been Madame Elisabeth's confessor, but had not previously ministered to the King, had been named to the authorities as the priest whom Louis wished to see. He was allowed to say Mass and to do his holy office without objection. The abbé was admitted at the same time that Louis was officially informed of his own sentence. He writes of the condemned man, that he was 'calm, tranquil, and even gracious. Not one of those who stood about him had as assured an air as his.' Taking M. de Firmont into his cabinet when the deputation had gone, the King was for a moment unmanned by the grief of his loyal subject, but he presently said, 'The great affair, the only one—for what are all other affairs in comparison?—must entirely occupy me, yet I ask a few minutes delay, for my family are coming down to me.' At eight o'clock they were announced, after long expectation, during which Louis conversed on political subjects. The Abbé Edgeworth retired to the cabinet adjoining, from whence he necessarily heard what passed.

CHAPTER XI.

Louis the Sixteenth on the Scaffold.

LOUIS XVI. bidding adieu to his family the night before his execution has been often painted whether on canvas or in the pages of history. The farewell was said in the dining-room of the King's apartments, the door of which had glass panes, so that the movements of the prisoners might be seen by the municipals. There the King awaited impatiently the coming of his family. The Queen entered first, leading her son, and followed by Madame Elisabeth and Madame Royale. Silence, broken only by sobs, accompanied the strong embraces of parents and children. Then the King sat down, his wife and sister at his left and right, his daughter before him; the young Prince stood between his father's knees. All leant towards him and often kissed him. For an hour and three quarters the attendants watched their anguish. The King was the chief speaker. 'He related his trial to my mother,' writes Madame Royale, 'excusing the wretches who caused his death. He then gave religious instructions to my brother, desiring him particularly to forgive those who had brought about his death, and he gave to him his blessing as well as to me.' At a quarter past ten Louis rose, and the others followed him with bitter lamentations. Clery opened the door. The Queen held the King by the right arm and both held the Dauphin by the hand. Madame Royale's arms were round her father's waist, and Madame Elisabeth clung to the King's left arm.

'I assure you,' said Louis, 'that I will see you to-morrow morning at eight o'clock.' 'You promise?' they all said together. 'Yes, I promise.' 'Why not at seven?' asked the Queen. 'Well then at seven,' replied the King. 'Farewell!'

Madame Royale, fainting, had to be supported to her room in the rough arms of the guards, while in their agony of grief, too vehement for form or articulation, the wife, son, and sister were hustled back to their prison.

'Ah,' exclaimed the King in over-mastering agitation to his confessor; 'the cruel sacrifice is made, help me, sir, now to forget all but my salvation; that must henceforward occupy my heart and thoughts.' The King, when it was time, supped with fair appetite, after that he remained till half-past twelve on his knees. Then, by the Abbé Edgeworth's advice, he went to bed, and he slept calmly till five o'clock. Mass was said, and during it the King made his last communion. Some trifling kindnesses to be done for Clery, afterwards engaged his attention, and presently the abbé rejoining him found him warming himself by the stove. 'How fortunate I am to be sure of my principles,' observed the King. 'Without them, how would it now be with me? but possessed of them death should seem sweet to me. Yes, there is above an incorruptible Judge who will render me the justice I am refused by men.' When day broke, he listened quietly to the noise of preparation among the National Guard. He was heard often to murmur, 'I change a corruptible for an incorruptible crown.'

Faithful to his word, he wished to see once more his family, but the Abbé Edgeworth prayed him to abstain from an interview that might kill the Queen. Louis sorrowfully agreed, then taking Clery aside, he gave him a ring for his son, and a seal for the Queen. 'Tell her,' he said, 'that I leave her with difficulty. This little packet contains some hair of all the members of my family. Give it also to her.' In a most sorrowful voice he added, 'I charge you to bid them farewell.' Afterwards he asked for the blessing and prayers of his confessor, that he might have strength to the end. The officials who came to summon him having their hats on, he also put on his, as he said with firmness, 'Let us go.'

On his way to execution he read the psalms for the dying in the Abbé Edgeworth's breviary. When arrived at the foot of the scaffold, he undid his cravat and untied his hair, as was required, himself. But he at first refused to allow the executioners to bind his arms. He looked as if for advice to his confessor. 'Sire,' said the priest, 'it is but another point in which you resemble that God who is about to be your reward.'

'As you will,' said the King. 'I will drink the cup to the dregs.'

Louis had so often proved his power of self-control, and showed undaunted calmness, that it is entirely improbable that, as has been said, he should have failed in dignity on the scaffold. But as he has been accused even of personal violence towards his executioners, it is perhaps worth while to translate the letter of Sanson, the headsman, which was addressed within a month of the event, to the *Thermomètre*, a newspaper which had published a false account of the King's death.

'Paris, February 20, 1793. Year II. of the French Republic.

'A short journey has been the cause why I have not had the honour of replying to the request you made me in your journal on the subject of Louis Capet.

Here is, according to my promise, the exact truth of what happened. Getting down from the carriage for the execution, he was told that he must take off his coat. He made some difficulties, saying that he might be executed as he was. When it was represented to him that the thing was impossible, he himself helped to take off his coat. He made the same difficulty when it was necessary to tie his hands, which he offered himself when the person who was with him (the Abbé Edgeworth) told him that it was a last sacrifice. Then he inquired if the drums would continue beating; he was told that no one knew, and that was the truth. He ascended the scaffold and tried to come forward as if he would speak, but he was informed that this also was impossible, and he let himself be led to the place where he was tied. From there he cried very loudly : "People, I die innocent;" then turning towards us he said to us, "Gentlemen, I am innocent of all that I am accused of; I desire that my blood may cement the welfare of the French people." These, citizen, were his last and true words. The little debate which happened at the foot of the scaffold turned on his not having believed it to be necessary that his coat should be taken off and his hands tied. He also proposed to cut off his hair himself.

'And, to render homage to truth, he bore all this with a coolness and firmness that surprized us all. I am quite convinced that he drew this firmness from his religious principles—no one could seem more influenced by them than he did, or more certain of them.

'You may rest assured, citizen, that this is the entire truth.

'I have the honour to be, citizen,

'Your fellow-citizen,

'SANSON.'

The body of the King, dressed as he was, was carried away in a wicker basket, and buried in the old cemetery of the Church of the Madeleine de la Ville d'Evêque, with sufficient quick-lime to destroy as soon as might be the last relics of the last monarch of old France. Many of the by-standers dabbled their hands and marked their faces in his blood; for had not public opinion declared him a tyrant, and did not a hundred and thirty-three newspapers and an incredible number of pamphlets aver that he was guilty of the nation's miseries? Just twenty-two years after this, the same public opinion proclaimed that the doubtful fragments of bone found where Louis had been buried were worthy of all the honour that a repentant people could pay; and a gilt inscription on the coffin in which they were placed announced that Capet of the Temple was once more 'the most high, most powerful, and most excellent Prince, by the grace of God, King of France and of Navarre.'

'Barrère's saying, "Only they who are dead never return,"' has been too much quoted,' writes M. Louis Blanc. 'The contrary is true, and it is only the dead who do return.' 'The republicans did not guess,' he elsewhere observes, 'how dangerous to their cause would be the legend of a King who was supposed to be a martyr.'

CHAPTER XII.

The Heir to the Throne.

THE Courts of Europe, except that of Madrid, had done little to avert the blow which in the person of Louis had fallen on all the crowned heads of the West. But the horror which it produced strengthened the coalition against France. In England public mourning was ordered, and the French Ambassador was given his passports. Russia immediately accredited a minister at the Court of the Comte de Provence, who had assumed the regency of France, and ordered all French subjects to leave Russian territory. Prussia, Naples, and Spain, the Papal Court, and of course Austria, joined in a protest against the French Convention. Nor were the United States the least sincere of the protesters. There the funeral bells rang in all the parishes on the day when the news of the regicide arrived.

Louis XVII. was proclaimed King by the new Regent, and copies of his declaration were largely circulated in France, where, in Lyons, Toulon, Normandy, and the western provinces, the heir of Louis XVI. had faithful subjects. The Convention met by strong measures the threatening storms both within and without the French frontier. On the 5th of February, the suppression of all money bearing the royal effigy was decreed; on the 8th, the 'Septembriseurs,' guilty of the prison massacres, were excused from further prosecution on the 9th, the Paris militia was ordered to march to the frontier; on the 11th, all prisoners detained for bread or other riots, were amnestied ; on the 13th, the republican organization of the armies was decreed ; and on the 24th, a levy of three hundred thousand men was ordered. Now began that marvellous activity of the Convention, which in eleven months issued two thousand and odd decrees, and which defied with success the Coalition and the Vendéan attempt to restore the monarchy. But the death-struggle of the rival leaders of the republic had also begun. The radical differences in the schemes of the Girondists and Jacobins became evident when the republic had sprung into full being. The Convention was torn by jealousies, in its hour of strength, while the family of the Temple, in their captivity, grew to the full stature of martyrdom. The reign of the victim-King has significance for thoughtful students, careful of the meanings of history, as it balances the reigns of Valois and Bourbons faithless to their office when most powerful. Its short but miserable annals are written in unclean blood, yet they remain, perhaps, in their startling antithesis, the truest comment on the gilded error and wrong of those who laid the train of revolution. Louis the Great was the direct ancestor of Louis the wretched slave of atheist artizans and sacrilegious priests—of Hébert, leader of the Hébertists, and Marat, terrible even to his colleagues in his cynical ferocity.

Louis Charles, the second son of Louis XVI. and Marie Antoinette, was born at Versailles on the 27th of March, 1785. On the 8th of June, 1795, aged ten years and two months, he died in that upper room of the Temple which had been his father's prison. His agony belongs to history, for it is the culminating horror of the epoch in which he suffered, the furthest mark left on the sands of time by the tide of passion which

had overflowed France. The tragedy of the royal family
of France is crowned, as it were, by the sacrifice of a
victim in whom guilt was not only absent, but impossible.
The death of Louis XVI. can be at least discussed.
The hatred borne by an ignorant and maddened populace towards Marie Antoinette is conceivable. The very
piety and self-sacrifice of the King's sister, Elisabeth,
must have vexed to fury the readers of Père Duchesne,
for the large faction whose vices were fed by blood-
shedding would naturally not suffer such dangerous
virtues among them. And after all, death, even death
by guillotine in the face of an obscene rabble, is to be
borne, and the murder of a brave and believing man or
woman is not so extraordinary a crime that we need
recur to the tale of its commission with any extreme
astonishment.

The French revolt against the authority of the past
has been described by all manner of writers. We owe
to the period which may be marked off by the meeting
of the States General on the one hand, and the first
consulship of Napoleon on the other, a large part of
our sensational literature. The strained actors of 1793
possess a certain picturesqueness in their crimes and
in their heroism that commends both oppressors and
oppressed to our languid generation. Even the admirers
of Robespierre cannot but yield respect to Marie
Antoinette's seventy days in the Conciergerie, and
legitimist critics must allow a certain brigand distinc-
tion in Danton, and an heroic squalor about Marat.
And so, looking from a distance on the strife, we have
become reconciled to its horrible details. The world
has learned to excuse such outbreaks. ' It was expedient that he should die for the people,' has become
the habitual answer of conscience when revolutions
demand their victims. In 1793, as in 1871, the Reign

G

·of Terror accustomed us to strong historical situations. But no adult figure stands out from its red gloom with the same fearful significance, as the frail form of the child whose destruction seems to combine the frank cruelty of the middle ages with the meanness of modern murder. It is true that we do not sympathize with him as with the noble Queen and the little group of her faithful friends. There were far more dramatic deaths than that of the boy-King, but his history is important as a gauge of the deeds that may be committed in the name of revolutionary 'virtue.' As an instance of what the 'State' may do, no episode of the time can rank with this.

At the birth of Louis Charles, the second son of France, whatever may have been the factious disloyalty of the anti-Austrian party at Court, Paris was still eager in congratulation to the Queen. The affair of the diamond necklace had not, until the August of that year, filled men's mouths and ears with calumnies against Marie Antoinette, and when the news of her safe delivery reached Paris, there were the usual cannonades and rejoicings. The ancient ceremonial of welcome was gone through with creditable liberality, when the King came in state to Notre Dame for the *Te Deum* of thanksgiving. Fifteen buffets and fifteen fountains supplied the poor with bread and wine, and fifteen orchestras set them dancing until late in the night. The carmagnole had not yet become the fashion. The King was still the hope of the troubled nation, which looked to him to procure for them the visionary benefits promised by the quack philosophers of the time, and the hurras of St. Antoine were doubtless dear to his slow perceptions. The kind sentimentality of Louis XVI. gained for his wife an enthusiastic reception when, after her second son's birth, she drove to Paris to render thanks for her recovery. By one of the coincidences curiously common, if looked for, in men's lives, she dined at the Tuileries, supped at the Temple, and afterwards went to the Place Louis XV. to see the Spanish Ambassador's fireworks—an itinerary followed by her once more on her way to death. The little Duke of Normandy was scarcely more than four years old, when the death of his brother seemed to open for him an important future. The Dauphin, a boy full of intellectual promise, though weak and prematurely thoughtful, died within a month of the convocation of the States General in 1789. The son left to Marie Antoinette became the chief object of her life. From many sources we have his portrait, and charming as it is, the delicacy of frame, and the excitableness of temperament which the Queen endeavoured to counteract, are too evident to leave cause for wonder that the fragile child sank afterwards, morally and physically, under the persecutions of his gaolers. His recovery from the degradation of the Temple would have required the strongest testimony to be credible. At four years old, when he succeeded his brother as Dauphin, he is described as slight, graceful, and rather tall for his age. His brow was broad and high, but his arched eyebrows must have lessened its intellectual expression. His blue eyes were large and loving, his mouth was like his mother's, and he inherited her bright colour of hair and skin. Quick and agile in movement, there was a high-bred charm in his infantine ways which appears to have singularly attracted the roughs of the earlier revolution, but which excited the dislike and jealousy of its leaders after the monarchy had definitely fallen. He was courteous and affectionate, but impatient of control. His mother's intelligent devotion earned from him, baby as he was, a love and respect which never failed to influence him. 'Maman Reine'

G 2

was the object of his infantine adoration. His father does not seem to have gained from him the same frank affection, though it is hard to find a link wanting in the chain of duty and love which bound the King's family together during their captivity. But children judge keenly of character. They dislike reserve and weakness, and the sensitive Dauphin clung rather to his noble and impetuous mother than to the vacillating King. She personally watched over every hour of his day, even at Versailles, and herself educated his taste for music and reading. It is told of him that one day at St. Cloud he sat silent and motionless in his little arm-chair while the Queen was singing. 'For once Charles is asleep!' laughingly said the King's sister, Madame Elisabeth. 'Ah, my dear aunt,' the child replied earnestly, 'can one sleep while one is listening to Maman Reine?'

Contrary to the established custom, the King appointed no household for the Dauphin, that he might run somewhat less chance of the flattery which pursues a prince. His governess, until the emigration, was the Queen's personal friend, the Duchesse de Polignac. After her resignation of her office the Marquise de Tourzel was appointed to it, but the King undertook the superintendence of the boy's education while he was still in the nursery, for the child was hot-tempered, and resisted, while he was yet little more than an infant, the control of the women about him. Neither of his parents spoiled him. The royal family of France were learning from quickly following events, that austere self-denial, and the practice of fortitude even unto death, might be the most useful lessons that the Dauphin could learn. In the domestic anecdotes of Versailles, even before 1789, touching traces may be found of the anxiety of the Queen for her children's future. From the 20th of June, the day of the tennis-court oath, her clear sight taught her that the King's concessions could but end in disasters. From the moment that he abandoned his right of reigning to the third estate, France was no more than an arena in which the strongest conquered.

The Dauphin had not been long possessed of his importance as heir to the crown when he was called on to play his part in the scenes that followed the sack of the Bastille. Strange sights must have confused him, as the fear at Versailles grew with each new report from Paris. The secret flight of his governess, Madame de Polignac, and of his uncle the Comte d'Artois, the anguish of his mother when the King visited Paris against her prayers on the 17th of July, 1789, were lessons for him, baby as he was. While Louis was away on his perilous progress through the insurrectionists, the Queen's children never left her. The Dauphin, sympathizing with her, though he could hardly have known why, watched for his father's return from a window, that he might be the first to tell her. 'He will return, he will return,' the little fellow repeated ; 'my father is so good that no one would hurt him.' The King did return, wearing in his hat the tricolour cockade, the token of his humiliation.

Then followed the insurrection of women, the feverish life at the Tuileries, the flight of Varennes, the 20th of June, 1792. Danger and suspicion were within the palace, and royalty had become a mere scarecrow for insult and contempt. His parents mocked, his faith derided, the very foundations of his life torn up and ruined, what could the childish mind have thought, and the childish heart felt, among the raging eddies of the revolution ?

The incidents of his life necessarily influenced the Dauphin's character, and account to a great degree for the inequalities of temper, and the discrepancies of intellect which have been used in support of theories of his exchange for another boy. The combined wit and fear, the sensitive readiness and perception, and the resolute obstinacy of refusal in some trifles belong to his training when they are not distinctly hereditary.

There is no doubt of his almost precocious intelligence and his affectionate disposition. What must have been to him the ,phantasmagoria of the Tuileries and the Convention? The strain of the Temple life on his childish nature, in its extremes of virtue and crime, its noble courtesies and rough brutalities, must have been immense. It remains a wonder that his moral bewilderment was not greater still, and in the end his sad, uncertain backward glances to the nobler and lighter thoughts of his childhood are eloquent in testimony to the fine teaching of his parents and to the power of their example. Degrade him as his gaolers might, and distort his nature, the finely-tempered steel sprang back to something of its old grace and true position when free, and the racked and deformed boy on his death-bed faintly, but truly, echoes the thoughts of his parents.

CHAPTER XIII.

The widow and orphans.

MEANTIME, after the King's execution, the calm of desolation fell on the remaining members of his family. Shattered by the interview with her husband, which at the time she did not know would be the last, the Queen had lain dressed on her bed, shivering all night with the chill of grief. Her sister and daughter lay on a mattrass by her side. When the morning came, the noises without acquainted them with the preparations for the King's removal. Then the increased hurry announced his actual departure. The Dauphin broke from the group of imploring and agonized women, and ran from one official to another begging them to let him go out. 'Where to?' he was asked. 'To speak to the people, that they may not put papa King to death.' At last the cries of the rabble announced the death of Louis to his widow. She asked to see Clery, and hear from him the details of her husband's last hours, but her request was denied. For three days and nights she sat silent and sleepless, then her daughter fell ill, and the fresh care relieved her sorrow. 'Happily grief made me worse,' writes Madame Royale, 'and my illness occupied my mother.'

The captivity of the family became somewhat less severe after the King's death. The princesses were given suitable mourning, and when some alterations were necessary in it they were allowed to see the persons who made them, but only in presence of the municipal officers. One of the workwomen wrote afterwards to Madame de Tourzel : 'Monseigneur the Dauphin, whose age excused playfulness, asked me under the pretence of a game all the questions which the royal family wished. He ran sometimes to me,. sometimes to the Queen, to the two princesses, and even to the municipal on service. Each time he came near me he took care to ask me the question about the persons in whom the royal family were interested. He desired me to kiss you for him as well as Mademoiselle de Tourzel, forgetting none of those whom he loved ; and he played his part so well that no one could have guessed that he had spoken to me.'

When the paralyzing shock of the King's death had in some degree passed away, the Queen and Madame Elisabeth set themselves to fill his place in instructing his son. The lessons which Louis had given were resumed, even that in Latin, of which the Queen was not ignorant. In common with her sisters, the Archduchesses of Austria, Marie Antoinette had learnt the language of the Cæsars. She left touching witness to the fact in the words she wrote on a copy of the King's defence which had been brought to her—*Oportet unum mori pro populo*. There were plans made for the Queen's escape, but they brought nothing but trouble on the unfortunate family in the Temple. The municipal officers, Toulan, Lepitre, and Michonis were favourably disposed towards. the prisoners. A scheme was devised by General de Jarjayes by which it was hoped that the safety of all might be secured ; but the day before it was to have been executed the mob of Paris were excited to extraordinary suspicion and watchfulness by bad news from the seat of war on the frontier, and by a scarcity of bread. Delay became necessary, it was found impossible·

to rescue more than one person, so strict had the watch become as the terror grew on Paris.

When it was question of her flight alone, the Queen wrote to M. de Jarjayes—

'We had a beautiful dream, that is all ; but we gained much by it, since in this occasion I found again a new proof of your entire devotion. My trust in you is unlimited. You will find in me when they are wanted courage and character, but my son's interest alone guides me, and whatever be the happiness I might experience in leaving this place, I cannot consent to separate from him. As regards the rest, I fully recognize your attachment in all that you said yesterday. Be sure that I feel the kindness of your argument for my personal welfare, and I also feel that this occasion will not occur again, but I could benefit by nothing were I to leave my children, and when I think of this I have no regret.'

She said to Toulan with calm disdain, when he suggested that her trial would hardly be ventured on, and that her brother would demand her from the Government, ' What does it matter ! At Vienna I should be the same as I am here, and as I was at the Tuileries. My one wish is to rejoin my husband when heaven decides that my children should no longer need me.' Apart from sentiment the Queen was probably politically right. She understood her position in its full bitterness, and chose not only the noblest and bravest, but also the wisest course.

Toulan had been able to secure for the Queen the trifling objects left by the King in Clery's charge, and which had been sealed up by the Temple authorities. By the hand of M. de Jarjayes she sent them to Monsieur and to the Comte d'Artois with some words of farewell in

which all the family joined. Madame Elisabeth in vain
entreated the Queen to accept the means offered for
flight. For a few minutes on one occasion her eloquence
seemed to prevail. 'And you, my good sister,' said
Marie Antoinette, 'where and how shall I see you again?
It is impossible, impossible.' To Toulan she half apolo-
gized as she said, 'You will be disappointed with me,
but I have thought over it, There is in this place only
danger, and better were death than remorse.' 'I shall die
unhappy,' she elsewhere wrote to him, 'if I cannot in
some way show you how grateful I am.'

Even had she reached the German frontier, or La
Vendée, it is doubtful if Marie Antoinette could have
reaped benefits worth the agony of separation from her
children if left as hostages in the hands of the Convention. Her deliverance might perhaps have disturbed the
diplomacy of the Powers, just then occupied by the
partition of Poland. No pleadings of hers could have
altered the purposes of those who were, as they thought,
gainers by the French revolution. Better for her were
even the indignities of the Temple, better even the
terrible consummation of her sufferings, than the hypo-
crisies and heart-burnings which would have met the
Queen at the Court of the Regent, her brother-in-law.

The defection of Dumouriez, with other events, soon
directed fresh attention to the Temple. The precautions
against the escape of the prisoners were increased.
Tison, the attendant of the Queen's apartment, who
had been appointed by the Commune, was seized with
a fit of spite because his daughter was not admitted to
the tower. She denounced the municipals who had
shown respect to the princesses, and declared that she
had seen a pencil drop from the Queen's pocket, and
that she had found in a box some wafers and a pen. At
half-past ten on the following night, Hébert and several

officers of the Commune arrived at the prison. A strict search was made, but after three hours' labour no suspicious articles were found, unless it were some blotting powder and an old hat of the late King's which Madame Elisabeth had kept in memory of her brother. The more respectful municipals were dismissed for their want of *Civisme*, and better representatives of the Commune were chosen for the service of the Temple. 'I never heard of giving a table or a chair to prisoners,' said one of the new municipals, taking the young King's seat at dinner. 'Straw is good enough for them.'

In the beginning of May the boy fell ill. The Queen asked that M. Brunyer, the usual doctor of her children, might be sent for, but after long deliberation on her request it was decreed by the Commune that the physician of the prisons, M. Thierry, should attend the little Capet, seeing that it would be 'offensive to equality to send any other to him.'

The Prince's illness was troublesome. For some time he had complained of a pain in his side, and on the 6th of May he was attacked by fever and headache. There was reason for great anxiety about the medicines necessary for him, as on a former occasion they had brought on violent convulsions. At this time, however, the effect was favourable. 'He had only,' writes Madame Royale, 'some attacks of fever from time to time, and his pain in the side often.' But his health then began to decline, and it never afterwards recovered. The want of air and exercise had done him great harm, as well as the sort of life led by the poor child who, at eight years old, found himself in the midst of perpetual shocks, and scenes of continual emotion and terror. The sufferings of the boy, however, were of small interest to the nation while the downfall of the Girondists and the victory of the Jacobins divided France into hostile camps. Terror

and suspicion were gaining supreme power, and no man
thought of the Temple prisoners, except as possible
causes of danger. Rumours of any plot were sure to
be listened to by the desperate men who were in power.
The extreme watchfulness and *Civisme* of the municipal
Simon when on service in the Temple, earned the appro-
bation of his patron Robespierre. He communicated to
the Jacobin chief anonymous warnings which he had
received, or pretended to have received, of a conspiracy
for the removal of the prisoners. The Committee of
Public Safety readily believed the plot, and by two
decrees of the 1st of July, it was ordered that 'the
young Louis, son of Capet, should be separated from
his mother and placed in another apartment, the best
guarded of all in the Temple,' and also 'that the son of
Capet, when separated from his mother, should be put
in charge of a tutor to be chosen by the General Council
of the Commune.'

The attitude of the Queen towards her son, whom as
a last protest she had silently treated with some of the
respect that would have been due to him had he
been King, necessarily offended all good republicans,
and the diplomacy of Austria did not lessen her dangers.
At the Congress of Antwerp it had been decided that
the allies should seek 'indemnities for the past and
guarantees for the future' as the reward of their labours.
In short, the acquisition of a province was. a more
important end than the escape of Marie Antoinette,
and she might or might not, as the Paris factions
willed, be tossed a prey to the executioner, in proof
of a more excellent liberty, a more perfect fraternity.
And the sooner for the Queen the better, for the saddest
phase of her lingering martyrdom had been reached.

On the 3rd of July the decrees by which the Dauphin
was separated from his mother were executed. It was

nearly ten o'clock when six municipals appeared at the door of the Queen's apartment, and told her that her son was to be taken from her. 'Gentlemen,' she said, with difficulty checking the feverish trembling of her lips, 'the Commune cannot contemplate my separation from my son; my care is so necessary for him.' The order was repeated. In vain the wretched mother, and the aunt and sister implored respite, and wringing their hands knelt at the feet of the officials. 'What is the good of all this noise?' they said. But the Queen was desperate; she would not give up her son, and tried to keep the men from the bed in which he lay. They threatened to bring up the guard, and take him away by force. A struggle seems even to have begun, which awoke the boy. He saw what was happening, and flung himself into his mother's arms, entreating her not to leave him. The officials turned away to summon help, when Madame Elisabeth cried, 'Not that. Only leave him till morning, when he will be given up.' But the municipals were inflexible; they threatened the Queen so plainly to kill both her children if they were thwarted, that for love of them she was forced to yield. Madame Elisabeth and his sister dressed the sobbing boy, for the Queen had no more strength. But when he was ready, she took him and placed him in the hands of the rough, ignorant workmen to whom the Commune had given their misplaced authority. The child was wet with his mother's tears, for she felt that she should see him no more. But she gathered up firmness to entreat that the municipals should ask the Council for leave that she should see her son, if it were only at meal-times. Then the boy kissed his mother, aunt, and sister very tenderly, and went out with the men. The three women were left to their renewed desolation, to be embittered when the Queen

heard that the insolent shoemaker Simon, already known
by her as one of the most brutal of the municipals, was
to have the charge of her tender child. From that time
the courage of the bereaved Queen gave way. There
was no light in her eyes, no smile changed her set
sad features. Fortunately, after the removal of the little
Prince, the presence of a municipal in the Queen's
apartment seemed no longer necessary to the Government. The princesses were only visited three times
a day by the guard who brought them food. No
attendants were allowed to them. The hereditary
King of France was taken to the floor below his
mother's, where his father's apartment had been, and
left with Simon. He did not immediately recognize
the face of his new instructor, but by his voice and
manner he quickly knew his appointed master. At
that time of supreme anguish Madame Elisabeth was,
as ever, the strong and helpful angel of the family.
She did her best to shield the mother from knowledge
of the degradation that slowly gained on the unhappy
boy.   her

By the kindness of Tison, who repented of his
denunciation of the Queen, the princesses were told
from time to time how the Prince was. Through a
chink in the wall they even contrived to get distant
glimpses of him, as he followed Simon on the platform
of the tower, a sort of gallery which ran between the
roof and the battlement. The Queen, however, was
spared the knowledge of the indignities that her son
suffered until one day, after long waiting, she managed
to see him close, through the planking that divided her
side of the tower platform from Simon's. 'She waited
there whole hours to watch for the moment when my
brother should pass,' writes Madame Royale ; 'it was
her only desire, her only occupation.' It was on the

30th of July that the daughter of Maria Theresa first saw her wretched child in the Jacobin costume. The black he had worn for his father was changed for a 'carmagnole' dress of brown cloth and the red cap of the revolutionists. It happened that Simon was in one of his abusive tempers, and he pursued the boy with oaths and blasphemies. 'Simon had so terrified my brother,' writes Madame Royale, 'that the poor child did not dare to cry.' 'God has forsaken us!' cried the unhappy mother. 'I dare not pray any more.' But in a moment she recovered fortitude, and asked forgiveness from God and from her sister. Though she often watched at the same place she never saw her son again.

CHAPTER XIV.

Darkness and the Shadow of Death.

MEANTIME, the surrender of Valenciennes, the attitude of Lyons, and the threatening fleets of England before Toulon and Marseilles, created daily panics in Paris. In the Convention, on the 1st of August, Barrère wound up a violent report on the state of France by the words, 'Is it our forgetfulness of the Austrian woman's crimes, is it our indifference towards the Capet family, that has deceived our enemies? If so, the time has come to extirpate every root of royalty.' On the following day the Queen was removed to the prison of the Conciergerie, her trial was decreed, the expenses of her children were reduced to the minimum, and all tombs or monuments of kings were ordered to be destroyed.

There comes a moment in all noble lives when the character is especially tested, when the fine gold is tried in the utmost heat of the furnace, when the ordeal of solitude must be passed, and the soul must prepare in loneliness for its individual judgment. Then in desolation it learns to listen to the low whisperings of the Divine Comforter, audible at such times, and only then revealing to the attentive and listening heart the language of the lost fatherland.

Doubtless, airs from heaven crossed the threshold of the Conciergerie in which Marie Antoinette spent her seventy-five days of preparation. At two o'clock in the morning she was awakened and bidden to leave her sister-in-law and her daughter. 'She heard the decree read,' writes Madame Royale, 'without emotion, and without saying a word.' The princesses hurriedly begged that they might be allowed to go with the Queen, but they were refused. While she made a parcel of some clothes the officials stood by, and she was even obliged to dress before them. They asked for her pockets, which she gave up to them, and having emptied them they made a packet of the contents, which they informed her should be opened on her trial. They only left her a pocket-handkerchief and a smelling-bottle. She kissed her daughter, and desired her to be brave and to take great care of her aunt, and to obey her as a second mother. Then the Queen threw herself into the arms of her sister, and recommended to her the orphaned children. Madame Royale was so startled and in such profound grief that she could not answer her mother. At last Madame Elisabeth whispered some words to the Queen, and nerving herself to one last pang of severance the mother left the room, not looking any more towards her daughter lest her strength should fail in the parting agony. Leaving the tower by a low-browed door, and forgetting to stoop, she struck her head against the lintel. When she was asked if she had hurt herself, she said, 'Nothing now can hurt me;' and so, stunned by grief and the strangeness of her fate, she got into a hired carriage, with a municipal officer and two policemen, and was driven through the silent streets at early dawn to her Gethsemane.

By the help of M. Hue and Michonis it was possible for Madame Elisabeth to hear occasionally of the Queen, and by various channels information has filtered to the world without of Marie Antoinette's last weeks on earth. 'I observed when the Queen arrived from the Temple in the middle of the night that she had brought no clothes or effects,' is the record of a woman who was servant in the prison at the time. 'Next day and the following days the unhappy lady asked for linen, and Madame Richard (the female warder in charge of the Queen), fearing to be compromised, dared not lend her or furnish her with any. At last the municipal officer Michonis, at heart a worthy man, went to the Temple, and on the tenth day was brought a packet to the Queen, which she opened at once. There were in it three shifts, pocket-handkerchiefs, scarves, black silk or rock-spun stockings, a white dressing-gown for the morning, some caps and pieces of riband of different widths. Madame cried as she looked through the linen, and turning to Madame Richard and me she said, " By the care taken of these things I recognize the hand of my poor sister Elisabeth." '

Among the objects asked for by the Queen were her knitting-needles and some stockings she had begun for her son. The authorities, however, were, in her case as in that of the King, haunted by quite groundless fears of suicide, and did not let her have any needles. Work,

H

however trifling, had become to her an almost necessary relief, and she drew the threads of an old bit of
tapestry, and with two quill toothpicks she knitted a
strip of gartering. It came afterwards as a most precious
relic into the hands of her daughter.

Though one or two faithful and pitiful souls found
means to hint their sympathy, yet the hourly humiliations
of the Queen had little alleviation.   Bault, a friendly
warder, lent her Captain Cook's voyages, which she
read, doubtless not without memories of La Perouse,
and her husband's interest in geographical discovery.
What long ago dreams must have seemed to her the
luxurious pleasures of her Trianon—her 'little Vienna,'
as she had called her pet refuge from the Versailles
Court ! Which now of her subjects was in sadder
squalor than this 'daughter of the Cæsars?' Her gown
was worn to rags, her linen was changed but once in
ten days.   When, at her request, a cotton quilt was
asked for by her gaoler, Fouquier Tinville threatened
him with the guillotine.   And at last it was before a
jury of artizans and working men that Marie Antoinette
was brought to give an account of her life in all its
vicissitudes, and to hear evil constructions put on all
its perished joys and broken endeavours, its pitiful,
ruined royalty, of which the language was an unknown ·
speech to her judges.

But the utmost personal humiliation, the months of
deathful anticipation and sad grief might well be
borne by the brave Queen, strong in consciousness of
her goodwill in all the past, whatever undeserved constructions might be put on her hasty words and
impulsive actions. It remained for her, however, to
suffer the keenest anguish possible to a mother.   Her
son, degraded and vitiated as far as vice could lay
hold of his innocent childhood, must become the

mouthpiece of the supreme calumny which she was brought to endure. No one at any time had dared to say that Marie Antoinette merited even the simple doom of death. Robespierre, in the full stress of the hour and its see-saw of terror and crime, recoiled from the plot of Hébert to slay and defame her by means of her son. Yet, to those who confess the true meanings of sin and its revolt against God, no suffering will appear to compensate its malice; such will bow the head before the Divine retribution for the past of the French monarchy, and see in the Queen a victim ennobled, purified, and reserved for the prize of martyrdom; a victim that is satiated with the bitter savour of pain, but so made susceptible of a sweet reward even in her agony, which is unknown to souls on the lower levels of common life.

Those who endeavour to form any idea of Louis XVII. and his life in the Simon household, are indebted to the elaborate labours of M. de Beauchesne, who devoted himself to the task of its elucidation. He has not only patiently collected every evidence procurable in contemporaneous documents, but he has also had means of personal information which must be used by future writers who approach the subject. If he sometimes translates into too sentimental language the testimonies he has put together in his narrative, there is no reason to question their truthfulness in the main points, nor have his conclusions been disproved after much and minute criticism. On the whole, his details of the boy's life have been accepted as trustworthy history, and quoted as authoritative by men of opinions different from his. From three women who had been acquainted with Simon and his wife, M. de Beauchesne received himself the particulars which he has given to the public. One of these was an intelligent work-girl, who had seen

Madame Simon occasionally during the imprisonment
of the Prince. She had preserved some notes of her
friend's gossip about the Temple prisoners, and was
able to supply M. de Beauchesne with particulars of
the Simon tutorship as yet unpublished. As her relation
is perfectly consistent with known facts, there is no
occasion to examine her contributions to the history of
Louis XVII. in a hostile spirit, and M. de Beauchesne
is entitled to trust when there are no contradictions or
discrepancies in his story.

Antoine Simon was a journeyman shoemaker, fifty-
seven years of age. Before the revolution he had been
a tolerably good-humoured, though never a prepossessing,
man. He was sufficiently well off, for he had, in 1788,
married a woman of his own age who had been in
service, and to whom two small pensions had been left
by two of her employers. By birth she was an un-
educated peasant. Husband and wife were both short,
dark, and ugly in appearance, and both exaggerated the
dirty fashions of the republic. When the disturbances
of Paris began, Simon joined the Cordelier Club, and
became the fanatic disciple of Marat, near whose den
he lived. He was President of the Committee of his
Section, and by the favour of '*L'ami du peuple*' he was
recognized as a trusty instrument of the revolutionists.
His conduct towards the prisoners of the Temple earned
for him the approval not only of Robespierre but of
Marat. He was selected as the best available agent
in the 'management' of the 'little Capet.' Twenty
pounds a month was given to him in return for his
unremitting service, and his wife also was allowed £120
a year. She had, moreover, the triumph of a carriage
drive to the Hotel de Ville provided for her by sympathizing citizens on the occasion of her husband's
appointment.

It was late when his pupil was brought to Simon; we only know, of that first night, that the boy sat in the furthest corner of the room and hardly replied to the imperious questioning of his master. For two days he refused all food but a little bread, and during this time he was generally silent, though sometimes a flash of anger lighted up his features. He said to the municipals on one of the first days of his new condition, 'I desire to know what is the law which orders you to separate me from my mother and imprison me. Show me that law, I desire to see it.' 'Hold thy peace. Thou art impertinent, Capet,' retorted Simon. The poor boy's first resistance did not last beyond two days. After that he put himself to bed and dressed himself without further orders. He did not cry nor speak. 'So, little Capet,' said Simon, 'thou art dumb; I must teach thee to speak, to sing the Carmagnole, and to cry hurrah for the republic!' 'If I said all I think,' said the boy, 'you would believe I was mad. I hold my tongue because I have too much to say.' 'Ah, ah! master Capet has too much to say, that sounds mighty aristocratic; but I will form thee, I will teach thee progress and novelties!' One day Simon offered his pupil a jew's-harp, saying, 'Thy she-wolf of a mother and thy aunt play the harpsichord—thou shalt accompany them—what a fine row there will be!' The boy's refusal to take the toy gained him his first blows. They roused in him fiercer resistance. 'You must not beat me,' he said, 'for you are stronger than I am, but you may punish me if I am wrong.' 'I am here to order you, beast; I do what I like, and hurrah for liberty and equality!'

On the 7th of July it was reported in Paris that a plot for the liberation of Louis XVII. had been successful. A crowd of people went to the Temple to inquire if he were still there. The guard, who had not seen the boy since he had been in Simon's charge, did not give any satisfactory answer, and the ferment in men's minds increased so much that the Government thought it advisable to send a numerous deputation from the Committee of General Safety to verify the presence of the little Capet. The Terrorists were not so secure of their power as to be able to afford to despise the rumour of their prisoner's evasion. There is nothing in the instructions given to Simon on this occasion inconsistent with the temper of the men who were in power, and, besides, they were communicated informally—they were a shuffling hint, and not an order. Their improbability, which has been urged on the score of their cruelty, is disproved by the after treatment of the boy, which was in conformity to them.

'Citizens,' said Simon to the chiefs of the deputation, Drouet, the postmaster of Varennes, and Chabot, the ex-Capuchin, 'what do you decide touching the wolf cub—is he to be transported?' 'No.' 'Killed?' 'No.' 'Poisoned?' 'No.' 'But what then?' '*Got rid of.*'

The young Prince did not permit his examiners to leave without appealing to them to be allowed to see his mother, and desiring to know by what law he was so treated. 'Come, Capet,' said Simon, 'silence, or I will show these citizens how I "work" thee sometimes.' It is certain that from that time the cruelty of Simon was systematically increased, so that even his wife sometimes asked him to spare the child. The day on which he heard of the assassination of his friend Marat, drink and rage had driven Simon almost beside himself. He dragged the Prince to the platform of the tower, whence he could hear the murmur of the angry town. 'Cursed viper,' he said, 'thou shalt wear mourning for Marat; thou art not sorry he is dead.' 'I did not know him,' replied the child, 'but we desire no one's death.' '*We!*'

retorted Simon, 'dost thou pretend to talk like the tyrants thy fathers?' 'I said we for my family and myself,' replied the Prince. 'Ah, but Capet shall wear mourning for Marat,' repeated Simon, pleased with his own phrase; nor did he spare blows to increase the degradation of his victim. Yet Madame Simon reported to her former mistress, Madame Séjan, 'The child is a very dear and charming child; he cleans and blackens my shoes, and brings me my foot-warmer when I get up.' The Prince appears to have been obedient and even attentive, and not to have roused the temper of Simon, who, however, was invariably cruel to him.

Before her trial began, Marie Antoinette was doomed. Europe, hopeful of French dismemberment, abandoned her. Large sums were sent to Danton to bribe him in her favour, but Danton was himself on the fatal slope towards the guillotine and could not, if he would, have pleaded for her. Yet there was difficulty in finding evidence against her that could satisfy even the revolutionary tribunal. It had to be created; and the creators were to be Chaumette and Hébert, in whose special charge the affairs of the Temple had been placed. To suit their purpose, the Queen's son had to be trained, and no opportunity was lost by Simon to prepare him for the work that he was to do. His pure and frank nature was not easily degraded and broken down. On one occasion an infamous song against 'Madame Veto' —his mother—was given him. He refused to sing it. 'I will murder you if you do not,' shouted Simon, as he grasped a heavy andiron that was on the heath. 'Never,' repeated the boy, as he sprang aside to escape the iron which his master flung at him, and which would otherwise have killed him.

Blows and oaths would not have gained the end proposed by Hébert. Soon after the Queen's departure for the Conciergerie, the boy's habits were altered. He was forced to eat largely and to drink a great deal of wine, which he particularly disliked. Very little exercise was allowed him, so that he grew bloated and stupid towards the end of August. An attack of fever, which lasted for four days, occurred, and the medicine given to him altogether deranged his health. When he had partly recovered, wine was again forced on him; and when he was sufficiently tipsy he was brought to swear and sing as Simon and his boon companions among the municipals chose. To express pity for the child was to show 'moderation,' and any officials who had been guilty of that indiscretion were at once dismissed by Chaumette. Madame Elisabeth, who from her apartment could hear the cries of her nephew, persuaded a municipal to intercede for him. His remonstrance excited Simon's spite to worse excesses. 'Besides,' he said, 'I know what I am doing, and what I have to do. If you were me you would perhaps get on faster.'

Still, even in his degradation, the child remembered, though but in gleams, the light of his earlier teaching, and reflected it now and then in stray words, remembered for their strangeness by Simon's wife and her friends. One day the news of some Vendéan successes reached the Temple. The little fellow shrank into a corner, and waited quietly lest Simon should fulfil his threat of 'killing the wolf cub' in the event of a royalist siege of Paris. The 'mentor,' as Simon was pompously called by the Commune, pulled his pupil back by the ear, and put him in the middle of the room. 'Capet,' he asked, 'if the Vendéans deliver you, what would you do?' 'I would forgive you,' replied the boy, not unmindful of his father's dying commands.

In September, increased severity was shown to Madame Elisabeth and Madame Royale, and Hébert, with several municipals, visited their room. He told them that, among other changes, their food was to be given them through a trap in the door of their apart-ment, and that they were to clean their rooms and wait upon themselves. While the princesses were thus treated, the Prince was encouraged in excesses, which were made to alternate with prolonged fasts. Not only wine, but brandy was given to him, until his childish senses were dulled and depraved. A stolid indifference grew on him, he let himself be beaten without a word, he sang and swore as he was bidden, but when his mother's name was concerned, he could not be got to use bad epithets.

On the 3rd of October, the Convention ordered that the Queen's trial should be immediately proceeded with. To this decree the public prosecutor, Fouquier Tinville, replied that 'up to that day he had received no evidence relating to Antoinette, and that whatever might be the desire of the tribunal to execute the decrees of the Convention, he was unable to execute this decree as long as he was without such evidence.' On the 4th, Simon gave notice to Chaumette, the attorney of the Commune, that the little Capet was prepared to answer all questions necessary for the interests of justice. Simon was desired to be in readiness, and on the 6th of October the Mayor of Paris, Pache, Chaumette, and two members of the General Council, arrived at the Temple. The Prince had been somewhat before the time excited by brandy, and the effect passed away during the visit of his betrayers, though dulness and lethargy evidently benumbed him. Heussée, a police-officer, read aloud an interrogatory prepared beforehand (it is said by the ex-priest Danjon), to which the child was made to answer as he was required. When the reading was over, he was told to sign it. The fac-simile of his signature is in painful contrast with the fair copies written a year before under his father's eye, and sufficiently proves the boy's miserable condition. Hébert arrived as the treachery he had devised was being carried out by the attestation of half a dozen witnesses supplied from among the Temple officials, among whom, of course, was Simon.

'How on earth did you find out so many things, citizen?' Danjon was asked by one of his friends, 'and arrange the details so neatly and decisively?' 'I read them in public opinion,' he replied; 'they are clear as the sun.' The deposition of the child of eight years was, however, but doubtful evidence that Marie Antoinette was worse than a Messalina. On the 8th of October, Chaumette and his companions endeavoured to force from the Queen's daughter some expressions that could be twisted into confirmation of her unfortunate brother's deposition. She writes — 'Chaumette questioned me on a thousand wicked things of which my mother and aunt were accused. Notwithstanding my tears, they persisted for a long time. There were things which I did not understand, but what I did understand were so horrible that I wept from indignation.' For three hours the daughter of Marie Antoinette suffered the degradation of this interrogatory. The examination of Madame Elisabeth was shorter. No help in the frightful scheme was to be expected from her, calm and firm as she ever was in her truthfulness. The prosecutors were forced to rely for support of their accusation only on the first interrogatory of the Prince, which had been prepared by Danjon.

CHAPTER XV.

Requiem æternam.

On the 14th of October, the Queen was arraigned. She stood while the long indictment of her legendary crimes was read, and then sat down with calm in the chair placed for her. The previous day she had been secretly interrogated with all that ingenuity and cruel persistance in seeking grounds of accusation, which is a feature in French prosecutions, but calmly she had borne the test. Her accusers had acquired in their attack nothing but the shame of it, as they tortured her with questions on the most private thoughts and aspirations of her past.

She was dressed in mourning ; her appearance and manner were noble as in her splendour of royalty. The expression of her face was very sweet, but she looked around the reeking court, and on her judges, with so assured and serene a glance, that a woman who stood by exclaimed, 'See how proud she is.' Grief had whitened her hair, but she was still dazzlingly fair, and the crowd were quiet and subdued before the majesty of her presence.

But there was to be for her no respite. Enormous bribes had been offered to some of the revolutionary leaders. Danton had haughtily replied to the agents of the Comte de Mercy, 'The death of the Queen of France never entered into my calculations, and I willingly consent to protect her, without any view of personal interest.' But none the less inexorably did Robespierre's tool, Fouquier Tinville, spit his venom in the Queen's face.· Every unclean ·thing that had been but rumoured in court slums and the lowest tavern-talk was recapitulated. The epigrams of Monsieur, the idle jokes of the Comte d'Artois, the extravagance ·of the Polignacs, were brought against her, and with fatal effect on the minds of the tailors, wig makers, ·carpenters, and other working men who made up the jury appointed to investigate these matters. Still less, in the republican passion of the time, could they estimate fairly Marie Antoinette's political action. In her devotion to the King, her wish to preserve the monarchy, and in her natural, if misplaced, hope for help from Austria, were found reasons for her pre-determined condemnation. The witnesses produced against her had nothing to allege that her own unsupported explanation could not refute. With quiet dignity she unravelled the confused lies told of her conduct on several occasions. Men of the old Court, personal enemies, were brought from prison to testify against her, but their testimony was favourable. D'Estaing, who had been among her enemies, contented himself with quoting a brave saying ·of hers when the mob invaded Versailles. 'If the Paris people have come hither to assassinate me, it shall be ·at my husband's feet. I will not run away.'

The Queen's singular good sense and ready power of thought, not less than her composed strength of mind, are proved in her replies to her examination. She had no hope in this world, but she remained serenely faithful to all the duties of truth and patience as if her life were to be prolonged.

'You taught Louis Capet the art of dissimulation,' said one of her judges, 'by which he deceived the people.'

'Yes,' she answered; 'the people have been deceived, but not by my husband or by me.'

'You desired to reascend the throne,' he continued, 'by trampling on the corpses of patriots.'

'We never desired other than the good of the people. We needed not to reascend the throne. We were on it.'

She was only careful in reply, and economical of truth, where the lives of those devoted to her were imperilled. These she protected with such subtlety as she possessed, which at one time indeed had been great. When accused of persisting in denial, she said, 'My plan is not denial. It is truth that I have said, and shall continue to say.'

The prosecution languished for lack of any one fact that could be proved against her, yet, among the various charges brought, Fouquier Tinville did not venture to use the evidence procured in the Temple; but on Hébert's interference it was read in court.

The Queen did not deign to take notice of it, and the president of the tribunal did not dare to press her for any reply. The audience, however Jacobin, was revolted by the accusation, but one of the jury having observed that the prisoner had not answered, the Queen, greatly moved, but with indescribable dignity said, 'If I have not replied it is because nature refuses to reply to such an accusation made against a mother. I appeal to all mothers who may be here!'

There was a murmur of applause in the court. Hébert dared not speak. Robespierre, when he heard what had been said, and the effect of the Queen's words, broke into an angry railing against Hébert's clumsiness, and even accused him of wishing to serve Marie Antoinette by the exaggeration of his charges. At half-past four in the morning, the torches being nearly burned out in the hall, the Queen received her sentence with unchanged countenance. She left the court without speaking, and when she returned to the prison-cell she wrote the letter to Madame Elisabeth, so often printed, and yet so noble a monument of a Christian Queen that it can hardly be too often reproduced.

' 16th October, half-past four in the morning.

' It is to you, my dear sister, that I write for the last time. I have just been condemned—not to a shameful death—that is only for criminals—but to rejoin your brother. Innocent as he was, I hope to show the same firmness as he did in these last moments. I am calm as those are whose consciences are free from reproach ; I regret profoundly that I must leave my children—you know that I lived but for them—and you, my good and kind sister, you, who in your affection have sacrificed all to be with us, in what a position do I leave you ! I have learned by the pleadings in my trial that my daughter has been separated from you. Alas ! my poor child, I dare not write to her ; she would not get my letter. I do not even know if this will reach you. Receive here for both of them my blessing. I hope that some day, when they are older, they may rejoin you and freely enjoy your tender care. Let them both think of what I have never ceased to teach them, that principle and the exact performance of duties are the bases of life ; that their affection and mutual confidence will be their happiness. Let my daughter feel that at her age she should always assist her brother by the advice which her greater experience and her affection will enable her to give. Let my son, in his turn, render to his sister the devotion and the services that his affection will prompt. Let them both feel, in short, that in whatever position they may find themselves they will only be truly happy in being united. Let them

take example by us. In our troubles what consolation we received from our friendship I and in happiness
there is double enjoyment if it be shared by a friend :
and where is a tenderer or dearer friend to be found
than in one's own family ? Let my son never forget the
last words of his father, which I expressly repeat to him,
' That he must never seek to revenge our death. I have
to speak to you of what is very painful to my heart. I
know how much grief this child must have caused you.
Forgive him, my dear sister I Think of his age, and
how easy it is to make a child repeat what is required
of him, and what he does not comprehend. A day
will come, I hope, when he will feel all the more the
great value of your goodness and of your tenderness.
I have still to confide to you my last thoughts. I wished
to have written them at the beginning of my trial, but
besides that I was not allowed to write, the procedure
was so rapid that I should not really have had time.
I die in the Catholic, Apostolic, and Roman religion,
in that of my fathers, in that wherein I have been
brought up, and which I have always professed. Not
having any spiritual consolation to expect, not knowing
if there are still here any priests of that religion, and
the place where I am endangering them too much if
they once entered here, I sincerely ask forgiveness from
God of all the faults which I may have committed since
I was born. I hope that in His goodness He will
receive my last prayers, as well as those which for a
long time I have offered, that in His mercy and goodness
He would receive my soul. I ask pardon from all whom
I have known, and in particular from you, my sister,
for all the sorrow which, without willing it, I may have
caused you. I forgive all my enemies the evil they have
done, and I here bid farewell to my aunts, and to all my
brothers and sisters. I have had friends : the thought

of being separated from them for ever, and of their sufferings, is one of my greatest regrets in dying. Let them at least know that to my last moment I thought of them. Farewell, my good and kind sister—may this letter reach you. Remember me always. I kiss you with all my heart, as well as these poor and dear children. O my God, how hard it is to leave them for ever! Farewell, farewell! I will henceforth occupy myself only with my spiritual duties. As my acts are not free, a [Constitutional] priest may be brought to me, but I here protest that I will not speak one word to him, and that I shall treat him as an absolute stranger.'

The letter is blotted with the unhappy Queen's tears. It never reached Madame Elisabeth.

A final charge the Queen addressed to her son —

'Let my son never forget the last words of his father, which I emphatically repeat to him. Let him never think of revenging our death. I forgive all my enemies the evil they have done me.'

Having finished her letter, which bears Fouquier's and other official signatures, Marie Antoinette flung herself on her bed, wrapped her feet in a counterpane, and slept calmly. At seven o'clock she was awakened for her execution, four hours before she had expected, but she was ready, for she herself had had her hair cut.

The Queen's passage to her death, among the 'dangerous classes' hired to insult her, is well known. Of the King's end it is easy to write calmly, but of Marie Antoinette's sufferings, borne with noblest piety, what can be said? The very imprudences of her Trianon career, the frank errors of her early queenship, the brilliancy of her youth with its rash friendships, its

misplaced generosities, the struggle she endured when
the royalty natural to the daughter of the Cæsars was
bit by bit stripped from her, serve to increase our pity
for the white-haired woman, patient and grave, who
slowly passed in a dirty cart along the streets of Paris
to the place of execution.

Twenty-three years before she had made her first entry
into the city, among an enthusiastic people, who could
not sufficiently admire and love her. Marshal de Brissac,
the Governor of Paris, had said to her, 'Madam, you
see before you two hundred thousand lovers;' and now
she was placed in a cart in which there was a plank for a
seat, while the carter with a lowering face led the strong
horse in the shafts slowly, for, as remarked a bystander,
'The Queen must be made to drink long of death.'

To estimate the contrast of what had been and what
was, the reader can glance backward and picture the
figure for whose triumphant passage soldiers had once
otherwise lined the streets. Of her, the artist Madame
le Brun, who several times painted her portrait, writes
with an artist's appreciation, 'Marie Antoinette was tall,
admirably made, rather fat, without being too much so.
Her hands were small, and perfect in shape, as were
her feet. Of all women in France she walked the best.
She carried her head gracefully, and with a majesty which
revealed her as sovereign in the midst of the Court,
though her dignity did not interfere at all with the kindly
sweetness of her aspect. It is difficult to render any
idea of such united dignity and nobleness. Her features
were not regular. From her family she inherited the
long and narrow oval, which is peculiar to it. Her eyes
were not large, their colour was almost blue. Her expression was intelligent and soft; her nose was well
cut; her mouth was not large, though the lips were
rather full. But the remarkable beauty of her face was

I

in its colouring. I never saw so brilliant a complexion. Brilliant is the correct epithet, for her skin was so transparent that it hardly took shadow. The last time I was at Fontainebleau I saw the Queen in her fullest dress, covered with diamonds, and as a bright sun shone on her she was quite dazzling. Her head was so set on her beautiful Greek throat that she had the imposing and majestic air of a goddess among attendant nymphs. I ventured to speak to her Majesty of the impression I had received, and of the noble effect produced by the way her head was set on her throat. Jesting, she replied, " Is it not true, if I were not Queen people would think I looked insolent ? " '

Marie Antoinette was but thirty-eight when she died ; but after her return from Varennes her splendid hair had suddenly lost its colour. Soon after she had herself painted for the Princesse de Lamballe, and underneath the portrait she ordered to be set the words, ' Sorrows have whitened her.'

Since then what furthest extreme of sorrow had not been hers ! And now soldiers again lined the streets for her passage, as in a triumph of another sort she went to her death, followed ·by the executioner, who held loosely the ends of cord by which the patient victim's hands were tied behind her. More than ever Queen, hallowed in the martyr-light, beautiful in the glow of the near dawn, as some thunder-riven mountain crest is beautiful, while all around is dark—Marie Antoinette serenely and gravely looked on the surging mob, many members of which were hired to insult her. She 'appeared indifferent,' it was remarked, for the bitterness of her desolation was passed, and the love for which she had ever yearned, half ignorantly—the sunshine and the glory in which she delighted—were at hand for her. Only the ingenuous salutation of a child in the arms of its mother could move her; the little one kissed its hand to her, and the Queen coloured as her eyes filled with tears. She had been almost in rags during her imprisonment, but her dress on the day of her death was neat and clean. There is a whole history in the inventory of the white muslin cap tied with an 'end' of black riband, and the white gown and kerchief which replaced the splendour of her Versailles costume. Her white hair was cut short round her cap. Her face, pale but for the hectic spots on her fevered cheeks, and her bloodshot eyes, witnessed to her agony. And Jacobinism was only the immediate instrument of her sufferings at the end of her life. They had been prepared by the Court of Louis the 'Well-beloved,' by false philosophies and rebellion against law under pretence of discovering new laws, by the collapse of her husband's authority, and perhaps most of all by the intrigues of foreign powers and by family treachery. 'There was in her death,' said the First Napoleon, 'something worse than regicide.' Regicide was not an invention of the age or the culminating evil of the revolution, but the calumnies that pursued the Queen, the accusation imagined by Hébert, were new in the history of crime.

Notwithstanding the exhortations of some ruffians, who tried to rouse against her the passions of the vast crowd through whom she passed, it was mostly silent. As she went up the scaffold she stepped by accident on the executioner's foot. 'Pardon, sir,' she said, 'I did not mean to do it.' When all was ready she said to him, 'Make haste.' To her, death was life.

CHAPTER XVI.

The Temple.

THE Queen's execution was not known in the Temple, but Simon guessed that it had taken place by the noise in the streets. He made a bet upon it with his wife, and proving right, he won enough brandy for a social evening, and did not fail to make his pupil join in the festivity. The boy-King had learned to bear the rough play of Simon and his municipals. As far as his injured health permitted, he was their companion in their cups, or their butt, as the whim took them. There was little difficulty in obtaining from him his now almost illegible signature to a denunciation of his aunt, which was wanted by the Commune. He declared, or rather Simon declared for him, that 'he heard sounds of knocking in the apartment of the princesses; that he also heard them go towards the embrasure of their window,, probably to hide something; he thought that perhaps they might hide false assignats, but of this he was not sure.' 'The sound was that of our backgammon,' writes Madame Royale, 'for my aunt, wishing to divert me a little, had the goodness to teach me the game.' Yet still some traces of his better life remained. He spent sleepless nights of remorse when he thought of what he had been made to testify against his mother and his aunt, and in his dreams old days were sometimes present with him. One night, early in January, he rose in his sleep, and prayed fervently on his knees. Simon awoke his wife to show her the superstitious somnambulist, and then flung a pitcher of water over him. The child, not being able to sleep in his drenched bed, crouched in a corner of it, and waited half stupified for what should come. 'I'll teach you,' said Simon, 'to get up in the night like a Trappist and say *Pater nosters.*' He took up his heavy shoe, and had just reached the bed, when the boy putting up his hands asked, 'What have I done to you that you should kill me?' With a push the 'mentor' flung him down in the wet bed, where the child lay trembling till day.

From that scene dates the complete success of Simon's system. His pupil fell into a kind of stupor, his mind and heart were broken—he no longer tried to please his master. It does not appear that Simon was in the beginning of his tutorship more than a coarse vain fanatic, but he was a believer in Marat and Robespierre, and did the work of the Hébertists. His new pride in liberty and equality urged him on to acts of the grossest tyranny. Probably the minute and harassing contrivances of the Commune for the close guardianship of Louis XVII. irritated him. Constant confinement— for he was ordered never to lose sight of his prisoner —told on his health and temper. He visited on the miserable boy his own vexations, and if, as was sometimes the case, his task revolted him, he became all the more brutal in his fanatical fulfilment of it.

On the 2nd of January, 1794, the municipal body decreed that no member of the Council could also hold any salaried office. Both Coru, the accountant of the Temple, and Simon, were affected by the measure. It was a time of theatrical action; the day after the decree was issued, Coru offered to resign his place that he might the better serve his country in the Council.

His patriotism was applauded, and 'civic mention' was awarded to him. The course taken by Coru made Simon's resignation imperative. On the 5th of January he gave up his well paid situation, and received the same honourable 'mention' as Coru. On the 8th, the Council of the Commune sent five of its members to the Committee of Public Safety to 'ask their wishes as to the nomination of the citizen who should replace citizen Simon as the guardian of the little Capet.' On the 16th, these five commissioners announced to the Commune that 'the Committee of Public Safety considered the mission of Simon useless, and thought that the members of the Council alone should watch over the Temple prisoners.' 'On the 19th,' writes Madame Royale, 'we heard a great noise in my brother's apartment, which made us think that he was leaving the Temple. We were convinced of it when, looking through the key-hole, we saw baggage being removed. On the following days we heard the door opened and steps in the room, and we remained persuaded that he was gone. We thought that some important person had been removed downstairs, but I afterwards was informed that it was Simon who had gone.

The partisans of Richemont, one of the pretended Dauphins who appeared after the Restoration, as also those of Naundorff, the claims of whose heirs were so eloquently pleaded by M. Jules Favre in February, 1874, assert that on the day of Simon's departure a dumb child dying of scrofula, the son of Baron Tardif, was brought in a toy horse to the Temple and substituted for Louis XVII. They pretend that the true son of Louis XVI. was carried away in a bundle of dirty linen by Madame Simon, taken to the house of Mdlle. Beauharnais, afterwards Napoleon's wife, and then handed over to MM. Frotté and Ojardias, emissaries of the

Prince de Condé, who had bribed Simon. The young King, as these ingenious supporters of Richemont and Naundorff declare, passed into La Vendée, where he was known to the chiefs of the royalist forces. He spent some seventeen months there, and in June, 1795, was sent to the camp of the Prince de Condé, who, a year later, confided the precious boy to the care of Kléber, the republican general, by whom he was made his aide-de-camp. This clumsy romance is supported by the alleged declarations of Madame Simon, who, when in the hospital of the 'Incurables,' where she died in 1819, frequently spoke of her 'little Bourbons,' and of her share in Louis XVII.'s escape. It is evident from the depositions of the nuns who received these declarations that, though not out of her mind, Madame Simon was liable to hallucination and extreme excitability, and it is probable that she had a morbid wish to astonish her hearers by a strange tale. Vague words at her age—for she was past eighty—are of no value without other proof. The supporters of Richemont's as of Naundorff's claim fall back on certain circumstances which they consider suspicious. They make much of the change of treatment pursued towards the child in the Temple after Simon's departure. Yet we have seen that it had already been proposed by the Commune to seclude the princesses almost entirely in the apartment above, and that from the first arrival of the royal family in the tower the jealous precautions against communication from without had been gradually increased. In the narrative which follows, our readers will find how entirely contrary to probability, and even to possibility, are the incidents of the Richemont and Naundorff romance. Who was Baron Tardif, the father who was found ready to sacrifice his son? Why, if Simon had been bribed, did he remain in Paris and die with

Robespierre by the guillotine? How was it that the Vendéan generals never used the Prince's presence among them during seventeen months to encourage the loyal zeal of the peasants? Why did the Prince de Condé on hearing of the death of the child in the Temple, if he knew him to be a substitute, issue a proclamation that ended with the words, 'Louis XVII. is dead; long live Louis XVIII.'? Why did the Paris Governments, whether Jacobin or Thermidorian, constantly act as if their prisoner were the son of Louis XVI.? How could so many of the Temple officials have been deceived? and if not deceived, did they join in the imposture? It is impossible to repeat more than a few of the objections to the Richemont and Naundorff story. Its incredibility will be shown by the simple relation of facts. It is true that there are at first sight difficulties in demonstrating the miserable truth of Louis XVII.'s identity with the boy who perished in the Temple; but there are impossibilities in the solutions which have been proposed in turn by each of the pretenders to the young King's crown of suffering.

The day after Simon's departure, the 20th of January, 1794, the report of the sitting of the Commune contains the announcement, that 'a commissioner on guard at the Temple informs the Council that Simon and his wife have handed over to the commissioners on guard the little Capet, and that they requested the commissioners to give them a discharge for him. The Council decrees. that a discharge shall be given to the citizen Simon and his wife for the person of the little Capet.' Chaumette and Hébert, who had always controlled the affairs of the Temple since the imprisonment of the royal family, accepted the decision of the Committee of Public Safety, that 'no special guardian be appointed for the little Capet.' They declared that they would adopt infallible

means to insure the safety of the boy, now that he was
to have no permanent gaoler. On the same day that
the Commune received the announcement of Simon's
discharge, the inner room of the apartment hitherto
occupied by the Prince and his 'mentor' was prepared
for the complete securing of the prisoner. The door that
opened from it on the ante-room was cut across breast
high, a grating of iron bars placed across the upper part,
and the whole was screwed and nailed fast. A small
trap was opened in the grating, so that food and drink
might be placed on a slab within the prisoner's reach.
What he did not want he was expected to return by
the same way. He was allowed neither fire or light
within his cell. A pipe was passed through the grating
which formed the upper part of his door, and thus,
whenever a fire chanced to be lighted in the outer
apartment, he could warm himself. A lantern that
hung outside the grating of his door was his only light
by night. By day the filtered and reflected light, that
retained but little sunbeam in its dim greyness, came
to him through the bars of the wooden blinds of his
closed window. It is difficult to realize the full cruelty
of the arrangement, but it was consistent with the
temper of the times, and with the terror and reckless
tyranny of the distracted Commune. There is no
mystery in the treatment of the young King, or in
his abandonment. Had he been old enough for the
guillotine he would have perished in that way; as it
was he was left to die by slow disease and decay; and
if there were calculation in the contemptuous neglect
under which he gradually sank, the changing factions
that decimated France cared little for its result during
the winter of 1793–1794.

At the moment of the boy's abandonment he was of
slight political value. Royalism was for the time crushed

throughout the length and breadth of France. It was in January, as we have seen, that the Government decreed that Simon should not be replaced, and that a special guardian for the son of Capet was unnecessary. In December, Toulon had been taken, and the English fleet successfully defied. Hoche and Pichegru had repulsed the armies of the Coalition on the Rhine frontiers. In December, the Jacobin proconsuls had stupified the provinces by their cruelties. The *fusillades* of Lyons, the *noyades* of Nantes, and the final destruction of the Vendéan army took place in December. In the whirl of death and terror during the winter, of what account was the sickly son of the forgotten King? As for the cruelty of his long solitude, cruelty was a virtue . of the hour. In December, we find Rossignol, the Republican general in the Vendée, writing to the Committee of Public Safety: 'There are yet humane men, and to my mind in revolution that is a fault.' And in December and January of 1793–1794, famine and frost were added to other terrors. The starving people forgot the remnant of royalty in the prison of the Temple. Even Chaumette and Hébert had other work on hand than the degradation of Marie Antoinette's son, for their fate was following them fast, as they came and went to and from the Temple, and gave directions for the living death of the boy they had ruined. The history of Paris during that winter is but the story of the struggle between Hébertists and Dantonists, and between Dantonists and the creatures of Robespierre. There is truly no mystery in the abandonment of the miserable representative of a forgotten dynasty, and on the anniversary of his father's execution, Louis XVII. was simply put away as the properties of some obsolete tragedy might be. In March, the Hébertists, by a strange irony of fate, were guillotined on a charge of planning the escape of the son of Capet, and the only acknowledgment of the boy's existence outside the bars of his nailed-up door was the occasional use of his name for mutual accusation among the contending factions. The slightest expression of pity for him insured the dismissal of the officers whose duty it was to verify his presence in the Temple. 'There was only one guard left,' writes Madame Royale, 'whose manner encouraged me to recommend my brother to his care. He ventured to speak of the harshness shown to the child, but he was dismissed the following day.'

It is hard to picture the condition of the delicate boy during the six months that he was left to rot in the gloom of his prison. No voice spoke to him, except when at night he was ordered to lie down, or called up to the grating for identification. He had been given a bell to ring if there were cause, but he was so afraid of the people about him that he never used it. For a time he swept out his prison and preserved some cleanliness, but his waning strength and courage made him give up one by one the last habits of a human creature. 'He lay in a bed,' writes Madame Royale, 'which had not been stirred for more than six months, and which he had not strength to make. Vermin covered him; his linen and his person were covered with them. For more than a year his shirt and stockings were not changed. No person cleaned away the filth that accumulated in his room. His window, closed by bars and fastened by a padlock, was never opened, and no one could remain in his room on account of the putrid smell. It is true that my brother neglected himself; he might have taken a little better care of his person, and at least have washed himself, since a pitcher of water was left with him; but the wretched child was dying of fear. He never asked for anything, so scared was he by

Simon and the other officials. He passed the day in doing nothing. . .'

What must have been the thoughts of his sick brain, as night and day went by, and fear was his only companion—fear, which is so painful even for a minute, and which haunted him incessantly? What phantoms sat by his rotting pillow, and pointed at him from the dim recesses of the place, and fevered him with the dreadful excitement of powerless abandonment? What terror in the streets could have equalled the terror of that delicate soul? All faith and love, all happy memories of his parents, had been taken from him, and he was left alone with the phantasies of his weakened brain. The scanty and coarse food supplied to him, the physical hardships of his situation, seem slight evils compared with the exquisite mental torture inflicted on him. The darling of Versailles, the dear son of his parents, was left to perish in a degradation that we suppose no foundling boy in France had ever suffered. The bright child, sensitive and imaginative above the average, was subject to an agony of solitude and darkness that no grown-up criminal can endure without loss of reason!

CHAPTER XVII.

Madame Elisabeth.

MEANTIME, without written or other evidence against her, the King's sister, Madame Elisabeth, was borne away with small ado in the dance of death. On the 9th of May she was taken from her niece, and next day she was sent with a batch of twenty-four to the scaffold, where she died with a pious courage and faithful zeal, so remarkable even in that time of brave Christian hearts that all present recognized in her a true child of St. Louis. Those who died with her confessed her their guide in the heavenward flight, and the crowd around knew that some rare virtue was present with them, and shrank in awe. That has been attested by more than one witness of the scene. Throughout her 'Path of Pain,' Madame Elisabeth is perhaps the most unspotted and touching of the revolutionary victims. Good common sense and a straightforward and consistent integrity were among her leading characteristics. She had the shrewd good humour of the best Bourbon type, and, fit accompaniment to common sense, she had a fervent piety and immutable faith, which lighted up with steady flame the palace or the prison in which duty found her.

She was left an orphan at three years old by the death within two years of her father and mother. She was fortunately committed by her grandfather, Louis XV., to the care of ladies who were, if somewhat rigid, not the less suitable to the task in such a Court as his. Her under-governess, Madame de Mackau, was judicious, and seems to have successfully repressed the child's very serious faults. Elisabeth was proud, obstinate, and hot-tempered, and the Court atmosphere fostered her bad qualities. She was indocile, and could stamp with rage when she was contradicted and made to learn her lessons. Gradually her good feelings were made to balance her impatience ; her reason was trained by discussion with worthy and well-informed persons ; and her violence and pride were transmuted into a firmness of principle and of purpose which stood her in good stead in the darkest passages of her life. She had not special wit or fascination, but she ever walked so straightly through the meshes of Versailles intrigue that not even the Hébertists dared to libel her, while leaders of the Revolution — Petion of the Gironde, Robespierre, the chief Terrorist—were moved to respect and pity for her. Many letters of hers, from those of girlhood to the secret notes written in the Temple, exist. In her correspondence with her friends her judgment is remarkably just. With fewer illusions than her brother or his wife, she steadily recognized the fate that was closing around the royal family, from the time of the summons of the States General and the admission by the King of new methods of monarchy. In almost every instance she judged soundly of those crises, when a greater firmness would at least have averted contempt from royalty, if it had not stayed the political cataclysm. Madame Elisabeth undoubtedly lacked the charm and the winning power of Marie Antoinette's nature, but, in that period of mixed frivolity and passionate thirst for social revival, the sober staidness of the Princess was a singular virtue. When the foundations of life were moved and the madness of Carmagnole and crime was

on the people, whirling away the old order with a *ça ira*,
her honest consistency in old faiths and customs is as
a clear beacon in the storm. By its steadiness it is
valuable, though eclipsed by vagrant lights and the
glare of more showy splendours. Madame Elisabeth
was but six years old when her eldest brother married
the beautiful Archduchess. Marie Antoinette soon
perceived the upright character of her little sister-in-law,
though it was still of rough exterior. In a letter to
Maria Theresa she says—'Since the departure of my
sister, the Princess of Piedmont, I know my sister
Elisabeth much better. She is a charming child, who
has wit, character, and a great deal of grace. She
showed, when her sister left, a charming feeling much
beyond her years. The poor child was in despair, and,
having very weak health, she was quite ill and had a
violent fit of hysterics. I confess to my dear mother
that I fear to attach myself too much to her, perceiving,
by the example of her aunts, how essential it is for
her good that she should not remain an old maid in
this country.'

Her first communion singularly altered Madame
Elisabeth; religious training bestowed on her a feminine grace and calm which at one time appeared
impossible for her petulant and brusque disposition.
Botany and mathematics were among her favourite
studies. An ingenious table of logarithms in her own
hand was preserved by one of her teachers, and, after
the Restoration, it was given to her favourite brother,
the Comte d'Artois. Le Monnier taught her the
properties and culture of plants, and Le Blond was
her master in history and geography. Not less than
Henri Quatre did she delight in Plutarch's *Lives*. For
her as for her great ancestor the old writer was *'l'insti-
tuteur de son bas age,'* and had doubtless taught her as

well, '*beaucoup de bonnes honnestetés et maximes excellentes.*'
Her style is very characteristic. Her letters are familiar,
diffuse, and incorrect, but full of freshness and confidence. Ingenuousness and energy, school-girl gaiety and
mother wit, abound in them, and she writes in the honest
old-fashioned idioms that suited her honest old-fashioned
nature.' She was perfectly tolerant for the weakness of
others, and indulgent in her household, but personally
she was careful to follow all prescribed rules of society,
and to respect prejudice that was harmless.

She was regular in spiritual exercises, and every day
she read the whole divine office and with it portions of
the best books of devotion. When she was seventeen,
her brother, the King, made her a present of a private
home at Montreux, a suburb of Versailles, and it was
as bright and happy as wise and pious practices could
make it. Her brother did not wish her to begin an
entirely independent life till she was twenty-five, but
though sleeping at Versailles she spent her time chiefly
at Montreux, generally walking or driving there with
some of her ladies after she had heard Mass in the
royal chapel. In work, exercise, and reading, the hours
passed until evening prayers, in which the whole family
at Montreux joined, after which Madame Elisabeth's
presence was required officially at Versailles. Her
allowance was not large, for Louis and his family
rightly recognized the poverty and approaching bank-
ruptcy of the nation. But the Princess did great things
for the poor according to her means, and rigidly forbade
herself all unnecessary expense. An ornament just then
the fashion was one day offered to her at a price of
sixteen pounds. 'But with sixteen pounds,' she observed,
'I can furnish two little households,' and the toy was
as usual refused.

She encouraged cheerfulness, and often supplied a shrewd and witty remark to her circle, but she checked gossip, and if she appeared at Court when any doubtful joke or broad story was being repeated, there was instant silence or the subject was changed. Her training and instincts kept her from sympathy with the prevalent philosophy. She was frankly royalist, and agreed with her brother, the Comte d'Artois, rather than with the King or Monsieur. But feminine reserve kept her political thoughts in the background. They only appear in her more intimate letters. Certain tendencies she loved or hated without reserve, but she was indulgent to the ideas of others. Only when the interests of religion seemed to her to be betrayed was she roused to unmistakeable anger. When her clear sight perceived the fate towards which the King was drifting, she acknowledged the danger, without alarm or alteration in her resolve to stay by her brother and his family to the end. In private she was not afraid to advise as her energy and faith suggested, and at certain crises of his life she remonstrated with the King for his irresolute concessions to public clamour. On the afternoon when the Bastille was taken by the mob, the Princess writes to Madame de Raigecourt—'If at this time the King has not sufficient severity to cause at least three heads to be cut off, all is lost.' 'I think,' she observes elsewhere, 'it is for governments as for education. "I will" must not be said unless one is sure of being right, but once said one should not give way.' Had occasion served, Madame Elisabeth would probably have been a woman of energetic action and capable of leadership. She was fond of riding, and we can picture her reviewing a valiant company of soldiers in the cause of faith and family right. All the more striking is her patient attitude at the Tuileries, when no entreaties of emigrant kinsfolk

J

and friends could move her from the King's side. In storm and sunshine she was faithful in loving ministry to him. Her aunts, to whom she was attached, wished her to follow them to Rome, but in a letter to the Abbé Lubersac, a chaplain attached to Madame Victoire, she writes—'There are positions in which one may not dispose of oneself, and such is mine. The line I ought to follow is so clearly traced for me by Providence that I cannot abandon it.'

She had been indifferent to the offers made for her hand by the Infant of Portugal and by her sister's brother-in-law, the Duke d'Aosta. Another, and in its spiritual significance a more brilliant, fate was before her. The humility that grew with her years was to have its fruit on the scaffold and not on the throne. 'It is really a pity that Madam should be so skilful,' said one of her ladies when the Princess had finished a piece of excellent needlework. 'It would be a more useful gift to some poor girl who had to earn her bread.' 'Who knows for what end God has given it to me?' replied Madame Elisabeth; 'perhaps some day I may use it to support me and mine.' While the royal family were in the Temple, and before they were separated from the King, she not seldom sat up to mend his clothes and those of the Dauphin—they had but one suit apiece—while in the official lists of their own linen during the months of their imprisonment, the entries of mended stockings, mended handkerchiefs, and other patchwork tell of the Queen and the Princess' industry. Madame Elisabeth was not beautiful. She had not the Queen's grace or dignity, and her nose was of the Bourbon type; but the sweetness of her blue eyes, her open countenance, and her smile which showed beautiful teeth, made a charming whole.

CHAPTER XVIII.

The courage of obedience.

THERE was much that was so different between her life and ideas and those of the Queen, that, while the old Court existed in its splendour, Madame Elisabeth and Marie Antoinette were rather good friends than companions. Montreux, the Princess' Trianon, was better known for its Swiss farm, its well cared labourers, its gifts of milk and fresh eggs to the orphans of the neighbourhood, than by the conventional Court entertainments. The changes of 1789 found her prepared, and she bade farewell to her emigrant friends, not many days after the Bastille was destroyed, with the presentiment that their parting was for life. The well known prayer to the Sacred Heart was given to her favourite companion, Madame de Raigecourt, in a last interview at that time. By its fervour and perfume of self-sacrifice, we know in what spirit Elisabeth passed from her peaceful home at Montreux into the region of storms. Henceforward her figure is generally present in all the troubles of the royal family, ready in council, patient in courage to endure, and rich in a practical good sense and cheerful wit, which supported not only herself but those around her, when the King's dejection and Marie Antoinette's broken heart might else have played their nobler qualities false. When La Fayette urged the King to obey the Paris mob which had taken possession of

J 2

Versailles in October, 1789, Madame Elisabeth was
against the plan, yet she said good-bye to her home
without a thought for her personal safety. During the
seven hours humiliation of the royal progress to Paris
she occupied herself chiefly with her nephew and niece,
and preserved a calm and almost indifferent air in
presence of the half crazy populace.

Attacks on the Church and its ministers were those
which Madame Elisabeth could least patiently suffer,
and vexation at her brother's weakness in yielding to
them makes itself now and then seen in her letters.
'Those who love God are so afflicted,' she writes, 'that
I begin to believe that the end of the world is near;
nor would there be any great harm in that.' When
the King sanctioned the Civil Constitution of the Clergy,
she exclaims, 'I see the persecution at hand, and I am
in mortal grief at the consent which the King has given.'
She breaks into joy when she hears how many of the
bishops and priests have refused to swear to the new
law for their organization. 'Religion has mastered fear,'
she writes, and she adds, 'I have no taste for martyrdom,
but I feel that I should be very glad to be certain of
suffering it rather than abandon the least article of my
faith.'

As the months wore on in the gradually narrowing
prison of the Tuileries, the external ministrations of
religion became first rare and finally inaccessible for
her. Her usual confessor having gone with her aunts
to Italy, she asked the Superior of Foreign Missions to
recommend her one. The Abbé Edgeworth de Firmont,
a name for ever associated with the last of the old
French monarchs, was selected. He came and went
with courage to the palace, and it was by his fearlessness
in discharge of his duty that he appears to have become
known to the King and Queen. On the 9th of August,

the day before the Tuileries were sacked, he spent some
time with Madame Elisabeth. For many months, during
which authority and government had slipped from her
brother's into, as she believed, unworthy hands, she had
needed all the spiritual consolation available. Frequently
she complains of the constant distractions which narrowed
her hours of prayer. 'You ask if I ride, and if I go
to St. Cyr,' she writes; 'why it is as much as we can
do to practise our religion!'

In the flight to Varennes, Madame Elisabeth played
the part of the children's maid under the name of
Rosalie. She is hardly mentioned in the many narratives
of that vain effort, and evidently kept so much in the
background that it is a surprise to find her talking
eloquently and most pertinently to Barnave and Petion,
the commissioners from the Assembly who were sent
to reconduct Louis to Paris. It must have been a
strange piecing together of the old and the new order,
when these missionaries of revolution, taking their seats
in the crowded carriage, were brought for hours into
familiar contact with the chiefs of the greatest European
monarchy. The shabbiness of the ladies' clothes first
struck Petion, arrogant and pedantic republican as he
was. He has left an account of his impressions whilst
in the society of the royal family. Passing by the offensive conceit with which he would have his readers believe
that he had awakened in Madame Elisabeth a personal
interest, his memoir casts an unexpected side light on her
intelligent good sense. 'I should be much surprized,'
he says, 'if she had not a good and beautiful soul,
though imbued with the prejudices of birth, and spoiled
by a Court education.'

Madame de Tourzel gives at length the conversation
held by the Princess with Barnave. An eloquent explanation of her brother's motives and the causes which led

to his flight from Paris wound up with the loyal words,
'I do not speak of our private troubles, the King who
should be one and the same as France, alone occupies
our thoughts. I will never leave him unless your decrees,
taking from me all right to practise the duties of religion,
force me to abandon him and to go to a country where I
shall be free in that respect. I hold more to my faith
than to my life.' When writing of the journey to her
friend Madame de Bombelles, the Princess with her
usual cheerful humour says, 'Our journey with Barnave
and Petion passed most ridiculously. You think no
doubt that we were very miserable. Not at all. They
behaved well, particularly the first, who has plenty of
wit, and is not as fierce as people say. I began by
telling them frankly my opinion of their doings, and
afterwards we chatted for the rest of the way as
if we had nothing to do with what was happening.
Barnave saved the body guards who were with us,
and whom the National Guard would otherwise have
massacred.'

Again, in a letter to Madame de Raigecourt, she writes,
'I am still confused by the shock we have experienced.
It would be well to be able to pass some days very
quietly out of the stir of Paris, to recover one's senses,
but as God does not permit this, I trust He will supply
what is needed. Ah, dear heart! happy is the man who
holding ever his soul in his hand looks only to God and
eternity, and who has no other aim than to use the evils
of this world for the glory of God, and so to profit by
them as to enjoy at last in peace the eternal reward.
How far I am from this! However, do not think that
my soul is given up to violent grief. No, I have even
preserved some gaiety. Only yesterday I laughed heartily,
remembering some absurd anecdotes of our journey, and
I am still effervescing.'

One at least of these reminiscences is probably preserved in Madame Campan's memoirs : ' M. de Dampierre had been killed near the King's carriage by the mob. A poor country priest close to Chalons was nearly meeting the same fate. He had the imprudence also to approach the carriage that he might speak to the King. The cannibals who surrounded it threw themselves on him. "Tigers !" exclaimed Barnave. " Have you ceased to be French ! Nation of brave men ! have you become assassins !" Only these words saved the priest, who had been already knocked down, from certain death. Barnave, when he spoke, had thrown himself nearly out of the carriage door, and Madame Elisabeth held him up by his coat.' Telling the story the Queen observed that at important crises strange contrasts always struck her, but ' the pious Elisabeth keeping back Barnave by the skirts of his coat seemed strangest of all.'

Madame Elisabeth was true to her race when personal danger threatened her. She was taken for the Queen by some of the mob on the 20th of June, 1792, and it was known that Marie Antoinette's life was in danger. Some of her well-wishers present exclaimed, 'You don't hear ; they take you for the Austrian.' 'Ah, would to God ! Do not undeceive them. Spare them the greater crime,' she replied. Turning aside with her hand a bayonet which almost touched her breast, she gently said, ' Take care, sir, you might hurt some one, and I am sure you would be sorry.'

A man in the crowd, who fell fainting close to her, she recovered by her salts, and those who witnessed this trait of courage and kindness in the midst of pikes and knives, were moved by it to goodwill. Who can say how far she altered the feelings of the populace, or how many crimes she that day averted. The attack seemed to miss fire and evaporate in strange flighty merriment.

A woman in the crowd said, 'Nothing could be done that day, our good St. Geneviève of the Tuileries was there.' The Princess had no illusion about the momentary reaction that followed. 'Fortunately,' she writes with irony, 'the month of August is near. Foliage being well developed, the tree of liberty will give a more certain shelter.'

Madame Elisabeth's last letter to the Abbé Lubersac is an interesting record of her thoughts two days after the June outrage on the Court.

'June 22, 1792.

'This letter will be rather long on the road, but I wish to let slip no opportunity of conversing with you. I am certain, sir, that you have felt as keenly as we have the blow which has been inflicted on us. It is the more severe because it is so heartbreaking and destructive of peace. The future appears an abyss from which one can come forth only by a miracle of Providence, and do we deserve one? The question takes away all one's courage. Which of us dare hope that the answer will be, "Yes, you merit one." Everybody suffers, but, alas, no one does penance; no one turns to God with his heart. How much I have to reproach myself with! Carried away in the whirlwind of misfortune, I did not employ myself in asking from God the graces we need. I leant on human aid, and I was more to blame than others; for who is as I am the child of Providence! But it is not enough to acknowledge faults, they must be remedied; I cannot do this alone, sir. Be charitable and help me. Ask of heaven, not that change of our circumstances, which, when God judges well in His wisdom, He will send us : but let us only beg of Him that He enlighten and touch our hearts. Above all, that He may speak to two very unhappy beings, who will be yet more so if He do not call them to Him. Alas! the Blood of Jesus Christ has flowed for them as much as for the anchorite who constantly bewails his most trifling faults. Say to Him often, "If Thou willest Thou canst make them whole," and plead by the glory He will receive in this. God knows the right remedies; but His goodness permits us to pray for all we need, and I avail myself, as you see, of this permission.

'I am grieved to write to you in so gloomy a style, but my heart is so heavy that it would be difficult for me to speak otherwise. Do not, however, think that my health suffers. No, I am well, and God gives me grace to be still cheerful. I hope that your health may be preserved. I wish I knew it to be better; but how is this to be expected with your keen feeling? Let us remember that there is another life in which we shall be amply compensated for these present sufferings, for, notwithstanding my extreme gloom, I cannot believe that all is lost. Farewell, sir; pray for me, I entreat, after you have prayed for the others, and let me hear often of you. It is a consolation.'

Madame Elisabeth did not share the Queen's hopes, or yield to the Queen's impetuous dislike of the men by whom it seemed possible that the King might yet be helped. When La Fayette, indignant at the outrages of June, returned from the army and offered his support to Louis, he was but coldly received at the Tuileries. 'Ah!' exclaimed the Princess, when he had left the room, 'do let us forget the past, and throw ourselves into the arms of the only man that can save the King and his family.'

But the Queen replied, 'Better perish than be saved by him;' and so it fell out, in sad truth.

The 8th of August is the date of Madame Elisabeth's

last letter to Madame de Raigecourt. She writes very briefly; but her good spirits were probably in great part affected to reassure her friends abroad. As 'the last dying speech of the "Executive's" sister' she congratulates her correspondent on the birth of a new citizen into the world. On the 9th, the eve of her brother's final dethronement, she writes in singularly playful style to Madame de Bombelles to reassure her on the attitude of the Assembly. Next day she made one in the procession of fallen monarchy, and M. de la Rochefoucauld, who was there, reports of the family—'The King walked firmly : his expression was confident, though grieved. Madame Elisabeth was the most calm ; she was resigned to all. It was her religious faith which inspired her. She said, seeing the ferocious mob on each side of the passage, "All these people are led astray. I desire their conversion, but not their punishment." The little madame (the King's daughter) cried quietly.'

Of the cells of the Feuillants' convent, where the royal family was lodged that night, Madame Elisabeth shared one with Mesdames de Lamballe and de Tourzel. She passed the hours in prayer, kneeling on the mattrass which had been put for her on the floor. Only towards morning could the Queen snatch some sleep, and, to keep it untroubled, Elisabeth dressed and quieted the children, and began those practical services and offices of tender sisterhood which were so helpful in the Temple imprisonment of her family.

Henceforth her life is blended with theirs in patient and united forbearance, and that union in faith, hope, and charity was cemented, which remains a pattern to all, and a rebuke to those who irreligiously disrespect family ties as a chief support in human life, purifying its joys and able to sweeten its bitterest sorrows. It would be difficult to ascribe too large a part in the

Queen's visible growth in patience and piety to Madame Elisabeth's constant influence, while the King freely confessed her services as the faithful angel of that sorely tried household. After her brother's death her gentle but unflinching courage nerved the Queen to constancy, and by her entreaties and advice Marie Antoinette once again roused herself to action, such as was possible, and to that hourly care of her children which could alone alleviate her sufferings.

CHAPTER XIX.

Ecce ancilla Domini.

It has been seen that from the clear and firm answers of Madame Elisabeth, when Hébert sought for ground for accusation against the Queen, nothing could be obtained. After the death of Marie Antoinette the seclusion of the princesses became stricter, and the last friend they could trust, Turgy, the kitchen boy, had been dismissed from the Temple on the 12th of October, two days before the Queen's trial. The last note that Madame Elisabeth found means to write to him is dated October 12, 1793, two o'clock.

'My child [Madame Royale] thinks that you made a sign to me yesterday morning. Relieve me from anxiety, if you still can do so. I have found nothing. If you have put it under the bucket the water might have carried it away, and it will certainly not have been found. If there is anything new concerning you, let me know, if you can. Were you able to read the second scrap of paper, in which I spoke to you of Madame Mallemain, one of my women ? This [a note] is for Fidèle, [Toulan]. Tell him I am sure of his sentiments. I thank him for the news he gives me. I am very sorry for what has happened to him.'

But there was no more sound from without audible to the imprisoned ladies, though pitiful noises from Simon's room reached their ears. They had seen the Dauphin's state, when called to hear his unhappy deposition, and were therefore not surprized, however grieved, when, after watching during two days at a little window from which the boy's exercise-ground could be overlooked, Madame Elisabeth saw him for a moment. The days went by in monotonous gloom within the Temple, but the powers outside were possessed by that unreasoning thirst for·unprofitable vengeance which would seem sometimes to follow crime. Day after day, during the winter and spring of 1793–94, the prison of the Conciergerie was emptied by the guillotine to be filled afresh from all the Departments of France. A conduit for blood had been specially excavated in thè Place S. Antoine for the service of the scaffold, the labours of four scavengers having proved insufficient. All thought of exile for the princesses passed away. In the hurry of the factions, the measure would have been too troublesome, though the Commune complained of their expense. Chaumette urged that they should be transferred to ordinary prisons, and it was meantime ordered that they should have no attendance, and nothing but the common prison rations. On the 12th of November, 1793, one of the gaolers complained, 'Madame Elisabeth would not salute me ; but she has to now, because passing through the wicket door she is forced to bow her head. I smoke my pipe, and send a mouthful of smoke in her face.'

Hébert seems to have felt a personal need for the destruction of Madame Elisabeth. His ruin and that of his faction, the most advanced of the men of the day in atheism and immorality, had been determined by Robespierre, but meantime, in the 'Père Duchesne' there was daily clamour that 'the last of the tyrant's brood' must be brought before the revolutionary tribunal. The Commune sought fresh subjects of accusation by which the Convention could be brought to decree the trial of the Princess. Her unhappy nephew was again made to sign a deposition against her, but it was clumsily prepared by Simon, and proved useless in its petty lies and details of impossible conspiracy. Simon swore that 'Charles Capet had been eager to bear witness for a week past' to their trivialties, but Fouquier Tinville could make nothing of them. It is said that Robespierre would have avoided the blunder of Madame Elisabeth's death, but at that moment, when the revolutionary chiefs were struggling for dear life, he hid his thought of reprieve under words of insult. 'He dared not claim that innocent woman from the ferocious impatience of Hébert,' writes M. Louis Blanc, 'without insulting the victim he desired to save.' He called her the 'despicable sister of Capet.' 'Such a word,' adds M. Blanc, 'applied to such a woman in the situation made for her, was an injustice, and, to be plain, a cowardly act.'

Hébert played with his wards of the Temple as if they were pieces in his game with Death and Hell. He and Madame Elisabeth were alike in their death by the guillotine, but which of them was in the sight of God and man victor in the eternal conflict? That those set grey days of winter and chill misery were to her the cloudy porch of perfection, no one need doubt who follows her to the end. Some precious words of hers are on record when cutting off a lock of her own hair she joined it with some of her brother's and the Queen's and gave them to her niece. 'Keep, my child,' she said, 'those sad memorials. It is the only heirloom that your father and mother, who loved you so well, can leave you. I also love you tenderly. Pens, paper, and pencil have been taken from me, so I can leave you nothing by writing; but at least, dear child, remember the consolations that I have set before you. They will take the place of the books which you have not got. Lift up your heart to God. He tries us because He loves us. He teaches us the insignificance of greatness. Ah, my child, God alone is true, God alone is great.'

Meantime, on the 24th of March, Hébert and eighteen of his friends furnished the guillotine with what was called its daily 'game.' Twelve days later, Danton, and a week afterwards Chaumette, were swept away. The Girondists, including Petion, had long since disappeared, 'victims,' it was said, of 'a generous Utopia,' but a Utopia in which divine law was forgotten.

On the 9th of May, 1794, at about seven o'clock in the evening, when she was going to bed, the bolts turned in Madame Elisabeth's door, and a rough voice cried, 'Citoyenne, come down at once. You are wanted.'

'Is my niece to stay here?'

'That is no affair of yours. Afterwards she will be seen to.'

Madame Elisabeth kissed the orphan, and to calm her said, 'I will come up again.'

'No, you will not return,' said one of the commissioners. 'Take your cap, and come down.'

'Be brave and firm,' she said with one last kiss to her niece. 'Hope always in God. Live by the good religious principles that your parents gave you, and never forget the last wishes of your father and mother.'

Then gently loosing Madame Royale's grasp, she followed Fouquier Tinville's agents, saying as she went, "Think of God, my child.'

While the receipt for her person was being made out and signed, she was searched. Then, in heavy rain, she crossed the court of the Temple to where a hackney coach was waiting. She was taken to the Conciergerie and kept until ten in an office there. From thence she was brought immediately before the revolutionary tribunal, and her first examination turned on some of the crown diamonds which she was accused of having removed for the use of her emigrant brothers. The remaining charges were mostly that she had been constant to the fortunes of 'the tyrant.' Madame Elisabeth spoke little, but with dignity. A friendly lawyer tried to say some words in her defence. He could have no speech with her, but hearing the questions asked of her, and her replies, he exclaimed that there could be no legal conviction when there were neither witnesses or documents produced against the prisoner. The president of the tribunal angrily accused him of 'corrupting public morality' by his interference. It was enough for the jury that Madame Elisabeth was the late King's sister. She was condemned to death before the sitting broke up, together with twenty-four other persons. It was idle for her to hope for any spiritual assistance, but her daily exercise had prepared her for all possible trials. The prayers composed by her, and so often uttered, bear witness to her saintly readiness for heaven with such eloquent testimony that here, while she is on its threshold, they may well be quoted.

'What will happen to me this day, my God, I know not. All that I know is that nothing will happen to me but what Thou hast foreseen, ordered and willed from eternity. That is enough for me. I adore Thy eternal

and impenetrable designs. For love of Thee I submit
to them with all my heart. I will all, I accept all, and
I make Thee a sacrifice of all that shall happen to me,
and I unite this sacrifice to that of my Divine Saviour.
I ask of Thee in His name, and by His infinite merits,
patience in my sufferings, and that perfect submission
which is due to Thee in all that Thou willest or per-
mittest.'

And now surely was ripened the fruit of that devotion
to the Sacred Heart of Jesus, which had been expressed
while she was yet of the world, in the prayer which she
had given to her friend Madame de Raigecourt.

'Adorable Heart of Jesus, sanctuary of that love which
wrought in God the will to become Man, to sacrifice His
life for our salvation, and to make of His Body food for
our souls; in gratitude for this infinite charity I give
Thee my heart, and with it all I have on earth, all that
I am and all that I shall do or suffer. And, my God, I
pray that this heart may no longer remain unworthy of
Thee. Make it like unto Thee; surround it with thorns
that may shut out all ill-regulated affections; fix in it
Thy Cross; may it know the value of the Cross and learn
to love it. Fire it with Thy divine ardours. May it be
consumed for Thy glory and be thine as Thou hast given
Thyself to it. Thou art its consolation in sufferings, and
the cure for its ills; its strength and refuge in tempta-
tion; its hope in life; its safety in death. I ask of
Thee, O loving Heart, worthy of all love, this grace for
those associated with me in this devotion.

'O divine Heart of Jesus, I love Thee, I adore and
invoke Thee, with my associates, all the days of my life,
and particularly at the hour of my death. *O vere adorator
et unice amator Dei, miserere nobis.* Amen.'

'It must be confessed,' said Fouquier-to Dumas, the
president of the tribunal, 'that she made no complaint.'

'Of what should she complain? Elisabeth of France!'
said Dumas ironically. 'Have we not surrounded her
to-day with a court of aristocrats?'

It so happened that of the twenty-four condemned, ten
were women, and of them two or three had been known
in the old days to Madame Elisabeth. Her strong sweet
nature asserted itself royally as she spoke words of comfort and hope to her companions. At that time the
state of the Conciergerie was so horrible that prisoners
awaiting their doom in its fetid and crowded wards were
often morally corrupted. As in a shipwreck, the evil
passions, the mean cowardice and egotism of men, over-
came ordinary restraints of customs and good manners.
Filthy dens, crowded with human creatures, reeling in the
intoxication of despair and in the near vision of death,
would have been anticipated hells, but for the light that
fell on some of their denizens from above, and which was
reflected by them on the shameful miseries around. As
the divine messenger commanding the gates of Dis to be
opened for Dante, Madame Elisabeth—

> Dal volto rimovea quell'aer grasso,

and by her countenance, radiant with faith, dispersed the
evil fumes of the pit that were thick about such doomed
souls as had no hope beyond.

One of the assistant warders has left some record of
her work among her companions, and has described
how the eldest there, seventy-six years old, was reconciled
to death, and could offer her short remaining span of life
with as much submission to the divine will as did two
young men of twenty by her side. Five members of the
Lomenie family were there included in the same summons, and to them Madame Elisabeth was a true servant
of consolation, even calming the mother who was about
to see her children die. Under her influence Madame

K

de Crussol, so physically nervous that a spider could in
old times have set her shrieking, bravely imitated the
royal leader of the little band, and with steady face
turned to the not distant light. That true helper of
souls in their agony must surely have had great joy even
then in her visible success. At last the time came that
the twenty-three, for one woman, being with child, was
respited at Madame Elisabeth's instance, should fill the
'living biers,' as Barrère called the carts for the service of
the guillotine. Madame Elisabeth sat by Mesdames de
Senozan and de Crussol d'Amboise, conversing with them
and encouraging them. As the procession crossed the
Pont Neuf, the handkerchief which covered her head
fell off. She remained bareheaded, and thus she attracted
the notice of many who might not otherwise have noticed
the calm sweetness of her countenance.

Lest any of the condemned should faint, a bench had
been placed for them by the guillotine, while they awaited
their turn, but the strength of none among them gave
way. The first called was Madame de Crussol, and
bowing low to the Princess, she asked with deep respect
to be allowed to kiss her. 'Certainly, and with all my
heart,' replied Madame Elisabeth. Each of the women
who followed received the same kiss of peace while every
man as he passed reverently bowed to her. 'Very fine
to salaam to her,' exclaimed a person below, 'she is done
for, like the Austrian.' Only by these chance words did
Madame Elisabeth know that the Queen had gone before
her. She repeated without ceasing the *De profundis* for
her companions as they died. She was the last. To the
person immediately before her she said, 'Courage and
faith in God's mercy.' And then she rose from her seat
to be ready herself when called.

She went up the steps of the guillotine alone, and then
looking upwards she left herself to the hands of the

executioner. The kerchief which covered her neck fell off as she was tied in the right position. A medal of the Immaculate Conception and a small key were hung by a silk string round her neck. When the assistant executioner tried to remove them she said, 'For your mother's sake, sir, cover me.' These were her last words. The lookers-on were silent, and there were no political cries heard in all the crowd. One who was there says he "fled away like the wind' from the scene of martyrdom, while Madame de Genlis, no pietist, and other writers of the day, agreed in saying that a perfume of roses was perceived in the place just after the Princess' head fell under the stroke. The bodies of the twenty-three were placed together in a common grave in the new burial-ground at Monceaux, which for two months had been used instead of the old ground of the Madeleine, now overfull.

Besides the sensible odour of sanctity which is said to have arisen from her mortal remains, her sweet influences rose as incense from the lives of those who had been her friends. Her sister Clotilde, Princess of Piedmont, was not far behind her in that perfection which was painfully acquired in danger and exile, and has been declared 'venerable' by a decree on the 10th of April, 1808, of Pius VII. Little prosperity attended the plans of those who came into possession of Madame Elisabeth's property at Montreux. The Government established a watchmaking factory for the use of the nation in her house, but it did not succeed, and Napoleon when first consul suppressed it. The old 'Maison Elisabeth' was sold for little more than three thousand pounds sterling to a private individual.

'Of what crimes,' asks M. Louis Blanc, 'could Madame Elisabeth's death be the expiation? What vengeance needed her execution for its satisfaction?

K 2

What need had the revolution of her blood?' Questions that indeed have no intelligible answer unless it be confessed that the world needed to be convinced of sin and of justice, and of judgment. Not for this holy and innocent woman need we sorrow, but for those who will not receive the lessons of her end. At thirty she was found ready, and if it be not given to man to say what was her place in the heavenly city, at least she is one 'of that white-robed army of souls to whom we look as guides to 'lead us on' when 'the night is dark and we are far from home.'

CHAPTER XX.

The orphans.

MEANTIME Madame Royale, Marie Thèrese Charlotte of France, remained alone in that upper room whence her mother and aunt had been taken for trial and death. Their teaching stood her in good stead, and she maintained herself in marvellous endurance through her long months of solitude and neglect. She was sixteen when left in this unexampled abandonment, and subjected to influences to which her resistance is as strange as any fact in the history of her family. She has left a memoir of her life in prison which is written with a dry exactness that makes it especially valuable, and it serves as a check on the loyal imaginations that are disposed to create legends and form myths around the obscure forms of the imprisoned children. The readers of her narrative, however, must remember that Madame Royale knew nothing of her brother, though he was in the room below, but what slight noises indicated, and what she was afterwards told by the men who succeeded Simon in his care.

When her aunt did not return that May evening, nor yet next day, Madame Royale asked what had become of her. 'She is gone for an airing,' the municipal on service replied. When she entreated that she might be restored to her mother, she was told that the Commune would consider the matter. 'One day,' Madame Royale writes, 'there came a man—I think it was Robespierre— he looked at me insolently, cast his eye over the books, and after having searched with the municipals he went away.' The young solitary girl did not speak to the chief of the Jacobins, but she gave him a paper on which she had written these words—'My brother is ill. I have written to the Convention that I may be allowed to take care of him. The Convention has not yet replied. I repeat my request.'

Poor brave child of sixteen, royally facing the spiteful Terrorist! The perversion of sentiment which distinguishes revolutionary epochs can alone explain the indifference with which the municipals on daily service in the Temple witnessed the slow destruction of the boy under their charge. It is true that they were only answerable for his body. Dead or alive, the presence of the Prince must be verified each day by the Temple officials, but if dead, the Convention would not have complained. If he were alive, and a word or action of his gaoler showed the boy pity, they might be brought into the fatal list of 'suspects!' Still the apathy of the municipals is a remarkable proof of the distorted principles of the time. Each night the commissioners of the day came to see through the grating of his door that the prisoner was safe, and to hand over the charge of him to their successors. At any hour they chose, the verification was made. Sometimes a longer scrutiny than usual took place, the lantern was turned full on the half naked, sickly figure within the bars, and dazzled and ashamed, the boy was called up to meet the scoffs of the patriots. He was never known to complain, even when his food came later than the appointed hour, when he showed his hunger by quicker eating. Sometimes he must have suffered painfully from thirst, as his strength failed and he could with difficulty reach the pitcher in which water was supplied to him. We will hope that the semi-idiocy at last produced in him was some relief. His passionate and brilliant intelligence became dulled as his will and spirit were broken.

Of this time Madame Royale writes—'The guards were often drunk, but they generally left my brother and me quiet in our respective apartments until the 9th of Thermidor. My brother still pined in solitude and filth. His keepers never went near him but to give him his meals. They had no compassion for the unhappy child. There was one of the guards whose gentle manners encouraged me to recommend my brother to his attention. This man ventured to complain of the severity with which the boy was treated, but he was dismissed next day. For myself I asked for nothing but what was indispensable, and even this was often harshly refused, but I at least could keep myself clean. I had soap and water, and carefully swept out my room every day. I had no candle, but in the long days, from May to August, I did not much feel this privation. They would not give me any more books, but I had some religious works and some travels, which I read over and over again.' There is a hint of bitterness in the sister's tone about her brother, that suggests vague resentment for the miserable depositions against her mother and her aunt that he had been drugged and coerced into signing.

The fall of Robespierre and the revolution of the 9th of Thermidor, or 27th of July, 1794, brought a change to the thing of skin and bone and sores that just stirred within the closed room of the Temple. The reign of defiant Jacobinism was over, the reign of frightened Jacobinism began, hardly less criminal, but more cautious, than the ' Red Terror.' The existence of Louis XVI.'s son might prove a useful card in the difficult game of the surviving Conventionnels, and yet his existence might become a serious danger for the republic. Perplexity and trimming are evident in the conduct of the Government during the remaining months of the boy's life. It was proposed by one party in the Convention, to 'vomit forth the infernal family of Capet from the soil of France ;' but another believed it more prudent to retain them in strict confinement. The dread of what might happen if the Prince escaped, and the risk of conspiracy if he remained in France, explain the cruel middle course that was taken with him, which only served to prolong his agony. At six o'clock on the morning of the day after Robespierre's downfall, Barras, who was one of the successful faction in the Convention, visited the Temple. He was in command of the anti-Terrorist militia, and it was his charge to go to the different posts of Paris and receive the new oath of fidelity required from the troops. With him were several deputies in full costume, and other officials. He ordered the Temple guard to be doubled, and recommended to the municipals on service the strictest watchfulness. In the *Memoires de Lombard* it is related that he went to the Prince's apartment, that he found the boy lying in a sort of cradle ; that Barras asked the prisoner why he did not lie on his bed, to which the Prince replied that he suffered less on the little couch. The author adds that he had on a waistcoat and a pair of grey trousers. As the trousers appeared tight, Barras caused them to be split open on both sides, and perceived that the boys legs were enormously swelled. He desired that a doctor should be sent for, and blamed a municipal and an attendant for the filth in which the child was left.

Though this story is in some points inconsistent with after facts, it gives valuable testimony as to the disputed points of the young King's power of speech. The supporters of Richemont and Naundorff assert that the boy found in the Temple on the downfall of Robespierre was incapable of speech, and his dumbness is the chief argument against his identity with the son of Louis XVI. The poor wretched creature, it is certain, seldom spoke, but it is very possible that Barras in military uniform roused in him some memory of the past, and untied his lips for the short answer to the first kindly inquiry he had received since he had been taken from his mother. In reply to other questions of Barras the boy was obstinately silent. The interview may not have been on the first occasion of Barras' reviewing the Temple guard, but on that day, as he left the place, he called one Laurent to him and desired him to wait on him in the afternoon.

Laurent was a man of violent revolutionary opinions, but he was educated, and well bred in manner. Madame Royale reports favourably of him, as very different from the drunken and brutal officials who had been her only visitors. He was only twenty-four, but his democratic principles had recommended him to Barras. He was a native of Martinique, and it is possible that his origin may have interested Madame Beauharnais and Tallien in his success.

'We have disposed of you without consulting you,' said Barras, when in the evening Laurent waited on his patron, and on the following day the young man received his nomination. The decree by which he was appointed is as follows—

'The Committees of Public Salvation and of General Safety decree that the citizen Laurent, member of the Revolutionary Committee of the Temple, is provisionally intrusted with the keeping of the tyrant's children detained in the Temple. The united Committees urge on him the most exact watchfulness.'

The decree is signed by seventeen of the revolutionary chiefs. A second decree orders that Laurent's salary should be paid monthly at the rate of six thousand francs, or two hundred and forty pounds a year.

On the same day he entered on his new duties. It was late in the evening when he arrived at the Temple. The municipals on service received him in the council-room, and conversed so long, that it was two o'clock in the morning before he was brought to the young King's room. Some rumours of the boy's condition had reached him, but his surprise and alarm were great when in reply to his call no answer came from the boy's bed. No threat or promise brought the miserable child to the grating. Laurent was obliged to accept his charge without further communication, but next day he applied to the Government for an inquiry. It was at once instituted, and on the 31st of July several members of the Committee of Public Salvation and some officers of the Commune came to verify the Prince's condition. They ordered the door to be broken open—a circumstance which contradicts the story of Barras' visit on the 28th, but which is consistent with a later visit. When some of the bars had been removed, one of the workmen thrust in his head, and seeing the child he asked him why he had not answered before. There was no reply. In a few minutes the visitors were able to go in. They found the child lying motionless on the squalid bed. His back was bent, his legs and arms were singularly lengthened at the expense of his body. His features were sunken, and he betrayed no interest in the opening of his prison; the torpor and indifference of a dying animal were on him! On closer examination his head and throat were found to be honeycombed by sores, long nails had grown on his hands and feet, his matted hair was plastered to his temples by dirt and vermin—there were tumours on his wrists and knees.

The sight of a boy of nine years brought to such shameful misery might well have moved even a philanthropist to charitable action, but fear was still so potent with the visitors that it was with difficulty that Laurent got leave to do something for his ward. Warm water was sent for to wash his sores, and with the consent of the deputation the prisoner was removed to the outer room while his own was being purified. 'Laurent had taken down a bed that was in my room,' writes Madame Royale; 'my brother's was full of bugs. He gave him baths and cleansed him from the vermin with which he was covered.' He even obtained leave that a surgeon should from time to time dress the boy's sores, and got for him a suit of slate-coloured clothes, a sort of semi-mourning.

CHAPTER XXI.

Last rays of light.

THE *Jeunesse Dorée* had begun to revive social forms in Paris, and *sansculotism* was forced to retreat before *Notre Dame de Thermidor*, as Madame Tallien was called, and her revival of luxury. Perhaps it was in sympathy with the new light, lurid and unheavenly as it was, that the little Capet's guardians changed their manners to him. Laurent insisted that the visitors of the Commune should cease to call him wolf and viper, and should address the prisoner as M. Charles, or Charles. But Laurent could do little in the face of the Convention, which remained unchanged in its hatred of the Bourbon race. He was not allowed, except at meal-times, to see his charge, and then only in presence of the municipal commissioners. The solitude of the prisoner was so little alleviated, that his persistent indifference and silence are not so strange as they would have been had he been encouraged. No doubt his coarse and scanty diet, which had not been improved, increased the languor and depression which nothing could move. One day Laurent obtained permission to take his ward to the roof of the tower. He waited to see what reviving influence the open sky and the distant sound of the city might have, but the child followed his keeper in silence. As he came down, he stopped before the entrance of the third story, where his mother'·

apartments had been ; he grasped Laurent's arm, and his eager eyes fixed themselves on the door, but he said nothing.   That evening he hardly touched his food. On another occasion, as he was on the 'platform,' a regiment passed with drums and music. He seemed to have forgotten the sounds, for he nervously seized his guardian's hand, but as the music continued to play his face brightened. Generally he looked upwards or straight before him as he walked, but one day he appeared to look for something between the flags and stones of the gallery of the roof. Some little flowers had thrust their weak stems among them. Long and patiently he collected them and made them into a little bunch, and when the time came for leaving the place, he took them carefully. When he and Laurent had got down to the door of the third story, the boy held Laurent back with all his strength. 'You mistake the door, Charles,' said his guardian. But he had not mistaken ; he had dropped his gleanings at the threshold of what had been the Queen's apartment. He thought her still there to receive his offering, as in the old days at Versailles, when each day he brought her a nosegay gathered by himself.

Before he had been in his painful and dangerous post two months, Laurent began to grow weary of his close confinement, and of the surveillance to which he was subjected. On the 19th of September, he addressed the Committees of Public Salvation and of General Safety, and reminded them that when he had received his appointment, Barras had promised him that on the following day a colleague should be given to him. 'Since then,' he adds, 'I have addressed several letters to you, in which I have explained to you the necessity of not leaving me alone in charge of the person confided to me. I have received no answer. Now that the atten-

tion of the Convention is drawn to the fate of the
tyrant's children, now that royalists are spoken of, and
that precautions cannot be carried too far, I feel it my
duty to reiterate my demand. I cannot suffice alone
for the functions required of me, and I think it is of
public interest that you should not lose sight of my
request. If at this moment any event were to take
place, I could not inform you of it myself. I therefore
conjure you, citizen representatives, to associate as soon
as possible with me one or two colleagues who will
share my watch, and who will answer conjointly with
me for the charge which you have confided to me.'

Not till the 8th of November did the Committee of
General Safety 'adopt and chose the citizen Gomin to
be associated in the guard of the Temple, and desire
the Section of Police to call him to his post.' On the
following day Gomin heard of his nomination. He
tried to excuse himself, but he was ordered to proceed
at once to his post. He was at that date thirty-eight
years old, a peaceable and worthy upholsterer, unmarried,
and without any near relations. A royalist gentleman
had by a nominally 'patriot' intrigue obtained his selection as a sort of guarantee for Louis XVII.'s safety.
Gomin lived until 1840 ; he served Madame Royale
faithfully, both in the Temple and after the Bourbon
restoration. M. de Beauchesne was personally acquainted
with him, and gathered from his recollections, still clear
even at the age of eighty, much of the information which
we · possess of the young King's last months. The
evidence of Gomin is so important in establishing the
identity of Louis XVII., that it has been made a chief
point of attack by those who choose to maintain the
'mystery' of his end. In a solemn affidavit used in
the trial of Naundorff's claims, and which was made
in 1837 by Gomin, he declares : 'Before his detention

I had seen the Dauphin several times and very near,
having been at that time commandant of a battalion of
the Paris National Guard in the garden called the
Prince's, at the Tuileries, where he was in the habit of
playing, accompanied by his governess, Madame de
Tourzel.'

In opposition to this is put an anecdote related by
M. de Beauchesne of Gomin's first interview with his
charge. On his arrival at the door of the Prince's room,
Laurent asked the new commissioner if he had seen
the boy before. 'I have never seen him,' replied
Gomin. 'In that case,' answered Laurent, 'it will be
some time before he speaks to you.' The sense of
'seeing' here is evidently acquaintanceship. The Prince
had never to his knowledge seen Gomin, and therefore
would preserve his habitual silence. But the fact of
Gomin's having seen the Prince at the Tuileries had
evidently nothing to do with the recognition of which
Laurent spoke. The general credibility of Gomin's
repeated and consistent affirmations of the boy's identity
is not, we think, shaken by M. de Beauchesne's anecdote,
and the readers will see cause, we believe, to be perfectly
satisfied of the old man's credibility.

It is said that thirty pretenders have in turn claimed
to be the ill-fated son of Louis XVI. To calculate how
many books and pamphlets have been born of the controversy on what has been called 'the Mystery of the
Temple' would be difficult. The most important work
on the subject is that of M. de Beauchesne, who has
devoted, he tells us, twenty years to the investigation.
The latest edition of his *Louis XVII.* is the most complete account of the sufferings of the royal family of
France in the Temple which has been given to the
public, and well merits the eulogium of the Bishop of
Orleans, with which it is prefaced. Perhaps M. de

Beauchesne has done wisely in leaving unnoticed the objections made by hostile critics to some of his assertions. He appears to have trusted to the mass of evidence which he has arranged in a flowing narrative as being on the whole too conclusive to admit of doubt. Still, though we are convinced of the general trustworthiness of M. de Beauchesne's history of the Temple prisoners, the questions which are suggested, as we read it, by some obscurities and contradictions, are very interesting. The objections made by those who assert the escape of Louis XVII. raise points which it is satisfactory to consider, if only because they invite us to examine the state of French society at the time, and the condition to which the outbreak of 1789 had brought it.

It was to be expected that, after the Restoration, claimant after claimant of Louis XVII.'s crown should present himself to the sympathies which were ready for his support. As each new pretender appeared, however, his friends had to clear his way, not only by endeavouring to disprove the existing records of the death of Louis XVI.'s son in the Temple, but by destroying the cases of rival impostors. The conflicts of the personators of the Dauphin have helped to lay bare every fragment of evidence touching his fate, until what was once a mystery has become sufficiently clear to any impartial mind.

In the first hopes and excitements, and amid the intrigues and jealousies, of the Restoration, the opportunities for imposture were too favourable to be neglected. Even during the Empire, Fouché had found it necessary to arrest one Hervagault, a pretended Dauphin, whose adherents were counted by thousands. Mathurin Bruneau, another claimant, was the object of an elaborate trial as soon as Louis XVIII. came to power. The astute King was glad of an occasion to cast discredit on all simulators of his nephew. It was rumoured, moreover, that there was provision made for the possible reappearance of Louis XVII. in the Secret Treaty of Paris. The position was one which readily produced a succession of pretenders. Many of the old royalists would have preferred as their King any other Bourbon than that Comte de Provence, who had had no small share in the ruin of Louis XVI. and Marie Antoinette. It was privately hoped by some of the veterans of the old Court that the promising boy of Versailles and the Tuileries might have survived the Temple. Much of the minute circumstantial evidence which has been supplied was not then accessible, as the rehabilitation of Terrorists and the idealization of Thermidorians had not then become fashionable, nor were the inquiries necessary for such processes easily made. The interest roused by Richemont and Naundorff, the two most plausible of the pseudo-Dukes of Normandy, was therefore not extraordinary. The 'Mystery of the Temple' was popular, and even so lately as in February, 1874, the pleadings of M. Jules Favre in behalf of Naundorff's heirs excited curiosity afresh. It is not many years since we have been reminded by an American writer of the claim of an Indian missionary, the Rev. Eleazar Williams, to represent the persecuted child of the Temple, while in dearth of other news, the *Times* now and then opens its columns to letters from claimants residing in this country.

Though M. de Beauchesne has left unnoticed the ingenious arguments advanced by supporters of the pretended Dukes of Normandy, he has, by his patient search for every record of the Prince's existence and end, collected materials for a correct judgment on perhaps the strangest crime of our age. He has searched every

remaining register of the Paris Commune and the revolutionary tribunals, the reports of the Convention, and
the archives of the Temple. He made himself familiarly
acquainted with the two municipal officers in whose
charge the 'little Capet' had been before and at his
death. He was even fortunate enough to gather from
three friends of Madame Simon some account of Simon's
tutorship and his wretched ward's sufferings. No guide
to the secret history of the Temple is so well informed
as is M. de Beauchesne.

His style is occasionally too sentimental for English
taste. In collecting his material from eye-witnesses he
possibly admitted some anecdotes that had crystallized
round the story of the child-King, as happens, consistently with perfect good faith, when history appeals
to the emotions, but time and its revelations has on the
whole corroborated his narrative.

Gomin and Laurent slept on the ground floor of the
Tower, as did also a third commissioner, who was
changed every twenty-four hours, and who was chosen
for duty at the Temple by each of the forty-eight sections
of Paris in turn. Very minute precautions in the service
of the Tower were still observed, nor do they appear
ever to have been relaxed. At twelve, the commissioner
for the day received from his predecessor the instructions
of the Convention touching his duties. After that the
permanent guardians brought their new colleague to
verify the presence of the prisoners, and to sign the
register of the Temple. The keys of the tower were
kept in a press in the council-room. The press had two
locks with different keys, of which each guardian had a
duplicate. They were therefore dependent on each other,
and the turnkey on both. Since the death of Louis XVI.
the Temple guard had been reduced to ninety-four men
of the National Guard, and fourteen of the Parisian

L

artillery. Passes to go out were never given at once to more than half the number by the guardians, and the cards of admission must be signed by both. Every evening a report of what had passed during the day was forwarded to the Committee of Public Safety. Each day, generally about nine o'clock, the two guardians and the commissioner went up together to the young King's room. Gourlet, a servant, dressed the boy in their presence, and, while he breakfasted, his bed was made and the room was arranged. A cup of milk or some fruit was usually his meal. Then the prisoner was left until two o'clock, when he dined in the presence of the guardians and the new commissioner. Broth, boiled meat, and a dish of plain vegetables, generally lentils, were given to him. Then he was left alone until eight at night, when a supper of the same sort as his dinner was served to him, he was put to bed, and, the lamp in the outer room being lighted, he was alone until next day at nine. With little, if any, change, the days and nights followed monotonously. Little pleasures were procured for his charge by Gomin, but very privately and cautiously. Four pots of flowers brought to his room seem most to have affected the child. He cried, and looked long at them, at last he gathered one. Yet for many days, he never spoke to Gomin, in spite of the kindness his new guardian tried to show him. At last he said : ' It was you who gave me the flowers, I have not forgotten.' And as the child began to trust and love again a slight colour came into his cheeks, and some reflection of his former bright beauty shone on his countenance. But it was a dangerous service to treat the innocent child even as well as the little criminals in a reformatory school would be now treated. The Thermidorians had replaced the bloodthirstiness of the Jacobins by a despotism and cruelty not less unscrupulous though more 'civilized' in its forms. A report read by Mathieu, a member of the Committee of General Safety, on the 2nd of December, sufficiently exemplifies the temper of the Government in its treatment of the 'tyrant's' children.

The *Courrier Universel* of the 26th November had observed that 'the son of Louis XVI. will also profit by the revolution of the 9th of Thermidor. It is known that this child had been abandoned to the care of the shoemaker Simon, the worthy acolyte of Robespierre, whose punishment he shared. The Committee of General Safety comprehending that to be the son of a king does not necessarily involve degradation below the level of a human being, has lately appointed three commissioners, worthy and enlightened men, to replace Simon. Two are charged with the education of the orphan, and the third is to see that he does not want for necessaries, as in past times.'

The Committee angrily repelled the charge of humanity.

'Citizens,' said Mathieu, 'I come in the name of the Committee of General Safety to give the most formal denial to the calumnious and royalist story which has been inserted lately in the public prints. The Committee is there represented as having given tutors to the children of Capet, who are shut up in the Temple, and having been almost paternal in its care of their existence and their education.'

He then explained the measures taken since the 9th of Thermidor (27th July) for the service of the Temple, and concludes—' By this explanation it is easy to see that the Committee of General Safety has only had in view what was material to a service with which it was charged, that no idea has been entertained of ameliorating the captivity of Capet's children, or of giving them tutors. The Committees and Convention know

how king's heads are brought to the ground, but they
do not know how the children of kings are to be
brought up.'

The remainder of Mathieu's report is a violent invec-
tive against royalist sympathies. It winds up by declaring
that 'the son of Capet, as well as the assignats bearing
his father's effigy, shall remain *démonétisé*—without value.'

CHAPTER XXII.

Eclipse.

THE attitude of Madame Royale seems to have maintained a steady dignity which repelled successfully the
boastful brutality of the Terrorists and Thermidorians.
Gomin describes her when he was first presented to her
by his colleague Laurent, as 'seated on the couch that
was against the window, and busy with sewing or em-
broidery. . She did not lift up her eyes or say anything
when Laurent introduced me. When I left the room I
bowed profoundly, and afterwards I knew that this
change from the usual customs of the place caused
me to be at once observed by the Princess. When
I saw her again, on the following days, I remained
respectfully silent, and I do not remember ever having
been the first to speak. During the first two or three
days of my installation she did not speak to me either,
but I thought that she watched me attentively, and when
later I witnessed her marvellous aptitude in divining the
political sympathies of certain among the officials, I do
not doubt but that her eyes quickly read my heart and
knew my feelings.

'Having the habit of shutting the door myself, I left Madame one morning, while my fellow-commissioners' backs were turned, some paper and a pencil, begging her to let me know by writing what she wanted. The first time she wrote, "Some shifts and matches."

'Gradually she gained more confidence and seizing favourable moments she ventured on a few words. Her feet being always hidden by her dress, her visitors had not observed that her shoes and stocking were worn out. It required serious diplomacy to procure some for her. None of those who saw her ventured to tell her any particulars of her family.'

While the existence of the wretched and half imbecile Prince was brought into occasional notice in Paris for the purposes of faction, some useless and mischievous attempts to serve him were made by foreign powers. Spain and Sardinia declared that they would 'never consent to treat with the French republic until they had obtained a satisfaction founded on the strongest sentiments of nature.' Simonin, the Government commissioner, who had been sent to Madrid to treat for exchange of prisoners, forwarded to Paris the following message : 'The King of Spain is disposed to treat on the following bases—first, Spain will acknowledge the French republic ; second, France shall give up the children of Louis XVI. to his Catholic Majesty ; third, the French provinces adjoining Spain shall form an independent State for Louis XVII., which he shall govern as King of Navarre.'

In reply, the Paris' Government ordered the instant recall of Simonin. On the 22nd of January, 1795, the Executive Committees presented to the Convention by Cambacérès their report on the proposition just made, that the 'Child of the Temple' should be cast forth from France. It has been said, on the authority of the

Comtesse d'Adhémar, who in 1799 wrote *Souvenirs de Marie Antoinette,* that Cambacérès had been privy to the escape of Louis XVII. from the Temple, and that he therefore was selected to report on the boy's fate to the Convention. In this narrative our readers will, we think, find that there is full evidence of Louis XVII.'s death in his prison, but certainly the able argument of Cambacérès in the debate on the boy's destiny, does not suggest doubt of his identity. He winds up his exposition of the situation by the words, 'There is little danger in keeping the individuals of the Capet family in captivity. There is great peril in expelling them. The expulsion of tyrants has almost always prepared their re-establishment, and if Rome had retained the Tarquins, she would not have had to fight with them.' The opinion of the Executive Committee was adopted without discussion, but all who knew the state of Louis XVII. knew also that the fate which the decision of the Convention implied for him was death. Their course, however, was cruelly reasonable. It was true that the presence of the unfortunate boy was an occasion of intrigue among the royalists of Paris, but his arrival at any of the European Courts, or in La Vendée, might have given a serious impulse to the plans of the emigrants and been a hindrance to the diplomacy of the revolution. The decision of the Convention was unsatisfactory to the guardians of the young King in the Temple; both of them were independent in circumstances and unambitious of their painful task. There was little for them to do beyond their regular duties as gaolers except to watch the slow but certain decline of their charge.

A violent storm of wind on the 25th of January caused some change for the better in the young King's lodging. The room he generally occupied became so full of smoke that, on the proposal of Gomin, he was allowed by the commissioner on service, one Cazeaux, to be carried down to the apartment of the guardians. He spent part of the day in the council-room of the Temple, and dined with the three commissioners. As usual, he was silent and uncomplaining, and seeing him so, Cazeaux said to the others, 'You told me that he was very ill. It does not appear to be so. Is it to excite interest in him that you have represented him to me as almost dying?' 'Dying! no,' replied Gomin; 'but in spite of what you say, citizen, this child is not well.' 'He is well enough, there are plenty of children worth as much as he is who are more ill. There are plenty who are dying and who are more wanted in the world.' Gomin, a timid man, was silenced, but Laurent observed that the boy's knees and wrists were greatly swelled, and told Cazeaux that the child suffered greatly from them, 'And if he does not complain,' added the kindly young man, 'it is because he is brave and feels that he is a man.'

The discussion spoiled the prisoner's appetite, though his dinner that day was somewhat better than usual. His eyes strayed indifferently about the room, while he crumbled a morsel of bread without eating or drinking. 'Why do you allow him to sulk?' asked Cazeaux. 'They say that Simon was rough to him, but no patience would hold out against his sullen manner.' Gomin put away a bit of cake for the boy, and left it in his room; but next day it remained untouched. The weakened mind of the poor child had understood and deeply felt Cazeaux's remarks, and it is singular that from that date his convalescence appeared checked. He was more subject to feverish attacks, and his joints became more swelled. 'My brother remained constantly before the fire,' writes Madame Royale. 'Laurent and Gomin urged him to go out on the tower for air, but he was hardly there before he wished to come down again. He would not walk, still less go up the stairs, his illness increased, and his knees were greatly swelled.' The rumour of his state got abroad, and it was even reported that the little Capet had been dead three weeks. The municipal surgeon who had been sent to see him, reported on his condition to the Commune. On the 26th of February, a deputation of municipals announced to the Committee of General Safety the 'imminent danger of the prisoner.' They were asked in what the danger consisted, and replied, 'That the little Capet had tumours in all the articulations, and particularly on the knees, that it was impossible to get a word from him, that he was always sitting or lying down, and he refused to take any kind of exercise.' They were asked the time from which his obstinate inertia and silence dated. The municipals replied that it was since the day on which Hébert had forced the child to sign the horrible calumny against his mother. We may regard this assertion of the Thermidorian officials as an innuendo against Robespierre and the Hébertists, whose tool Simon had been. The sullen avoidance of speech by the Prince would seem to date from his frightful six months of solitude and neglect. The case of a child left to rot, as he was, in darkness and foul air, is so un-paralleled that there are no means of judging of the physical and moral results probable in such a case. In the strangeness of the circumstances, who can object to strangeness of consequences as unlikely? We cannot say of the boy's persistent, though not absolute, silence, that it was impossible. The grandson of Maria Theresa may have had the obstinate will which is said to have survived the young King's struggle with Simon and with solitude. He may have inherited from his mother the pride which seems to have disdained help from alien hands almost to the last. The stolid apathy that fell

on him, the indolent sufferance that avoided risk of
speech and was little moved by change of gaolers, were
not unlikely traits in the son of Louis XVI. There are
certainly discrepancies in the evidence as to the young
King's power, or at least his habit, of speaking during
the last months of his imprisonment. It appears probable that the occasions on which he spoke were so rare
that a general impression of his absolute dumbness gained
credit among his municipal visitors. There was never
any question of his perfect power of hearing, or was it
ever thought that his silence proceeded from a defect in
the organs of speech. If we are surprized at his constant
refusal to answer the questions of the officials who examined him, we must endeavour to realize his sufferings,
the atrophy of which he died, and his natural repugnance
to the revolutionary visitors who had broken his heart
and ruined all his childish happiness.

On receiving the report of the Temple authorities,
the Committee of General Safety sent one of its
members, Harmand (de la Meuse), with two colleagues, to investigate the true condition of the young
King. The report of Harmand was not published
until 1814, and it therefore does not possess the same
value as if it had been given at the time of his visit.
Having at last reached the prisoner's room, after
unbolting and unbarring the several doors that secured
the dying boy, Harmand found him playing with a
pack of cards ; he did not desist from his game on
the entrance of the commissioners, or appear to notice
them. They spoke to him kindly, and proposed to
give him more liberty of exercise and any amusement
he might wish for. ' While I addressed to him my
little harangue,' writes Harmand, ' he looked fixedly at
me, without changing his position. He listened to me
with an appearance of great attention, but without a

word of reply.' In vain the commissioners endeavoured to move him. The boy looked at them with such an expression of resignation and indifference that Harmand writes, ' He appeared to say to us, " What does it matter to me? Complete your work." '

At the request of his visitors the young King showed them his hands, and, standing up, he let them examine his knees. ' Placed thus,' continues Harmand, ' the young Prince had the appearance of being rachitic and of defective conformation, his legs and thighs were long and thin, his arms the same, the breast was very short, the chest raised, the shoulders high and narrow. His head in all its details was very beautiful.' The boy when first requested to walk, obeyed; but he met a second order with silence and refusal; when scolded and threatened he did not show fear or surprise. ' His features did not for a second change. There was no emotion in his eyes; it was as if we had not been there, and as if I had said nothing.' It is hard to believe that there could have been a substituted boy found to play the part of Louis XVII. so well.

The commissioners, when they had left the Prince's room, visited that of his sister. They were warned by the guardians that she would not speak to them— nor did she do so, though her silence proceeded from less mixed causes than that of her unfortunate brother.

Harmand reports that she was knitting when he saw her, and her hands appeared to be swelled by cold. ' Madame,' he said, ' why are you so far away from your fire?'

' Because I do not see well at the fire-place.'

' But if a good fire were made your room would be warmed, and you would be less cold at the window.'

' I am not allowed wood.'

There was a piano by the bed, and Harmand observing that it was out of tune asked the Princess if she wished it tuned.

'No, sir; the piano is not mine. It is the Queen's. I have not, and will not use it.'

'Are you satisfied with your bed?'

'Yes.'

'And with your linen?'

'It is several weeks since I have been given any.'

The report of the commissioners was not followed by any improvement in the condition of the prisoners. The guardians of the Prince dared not on their own responsibility alter any of the severe regulations of the prison. The daily change of their third colleague brought constantly into the Temple the passions and agitations of distracted Paris, and the stranger municipals generally used their brief tenure of office with coarse assertion of authority. On the 23rd of March, we hear of one Collot who, looking straight into the Prince's eyes, said with an air of superior knowledge, 'This child has not two months to live.' Gomin and Laurent, afraid of the effects of his words on the boy's imagination, tried to explain them away; but Collot repeated with emphasis, 'I tell you, citizens, that he will be imbecile and idiotic before two months pass, if he is not dead.' On the 29th of March, Laurent asked permission to resign his onerous post. He had just lost his mother, and he was wanted for family business in his own home. It has been said that Laurent had been a party to the pretended escape of Louis XVII., and had acted under the orders of Barras. In the Naundorff lawsuit copies of letters from Laurent to the Thermidorian leader were produced, attesting the fraud, but they proved utterly valueless and were unsupported. Had Laurent been the agent of the party represented by Tallien and

Barras in any Temple trickery, he would have
demanded a reward; yet we find him in the following
year going to the West Indies in a subordinate capacity,
nor did he ever rise higher in the world than to be
secretary of the republican commissioner at Cayenne.
He died in that settlement in 1800.

CHAPTER XXIII.

Too late.

ON the 31st of March, Lasne, the new guardian appointed
in Laurent's room, arrived at the Temple. He had been
a house-painter in 1795. Before the revolution he had
been a soldier of the French Guard, but in 1789 he
had adopted the uniform of the newly created National
Guard. In 1837, when Lasne had just reached his
eightieth year, M. de Beauchesne saw him for the first
time. He received from him a sort of narrative of his
life, and among other incidents he informed M. de
Beauchesne that in 1792 he had had many opportunities, while on duty, of seeing the Dauphin. Indeed,
most of the people of Paris must have been familiar
with the features of the boy, either when he was in
public with his parents in their vain attempts to gain
popularity, or playing in the garden of the Tuileries.
Doubts have been raised as to his general credibility,
because in the trial of Richemont's claim, in 1834,
Lasne declared that he had frequently conversed with
the prisoner of the Temple, and because again, in
1837, he deposed in apparent contradiction to this,
that during the boy's severest sufferings no complaint

issued from his lips. Lasne went on to relate that one day, having presented a potion to the child which he hesitated to take, the guardian put it to his own lips, on which the sick boy cried out, ' You have, then, sworn that I should drink it? Well, give it to me and I will.' Lasne added, 'Those were the only words I heard him utter during all the time that I have spent with him.'

Comparing this anecdote with Lasne's repeated assertions of the young King's power and practise of speech towards the end of his illness, it requires little candour to see that by ' the only words,' Lasne meant the only hasty or complaining words. Besides, the depositions of Gomin are clear as to the occasional speech of his charge. The argument from the dumbness of the boy in the Temple in favour of his being a substituted child will not stand fair examination, and it is evidently founded on the report of Harmand and the rumours spread by municipals, to whom it is certain that the Prince preserved an obstinate silence.

Lasne appears to have had a stronger character than Gomin, and, from his entry to the Temple, he interested himself in the young King. In an affidavit taken in 1837, he declares, ' I had occasion to see the young Dauphin, the son of Louis XVI., at the Tuileries. I saw him again, and recognized him, at the Temple in March, 1795. I was intrusted with the guardianship at the Temple. The boy was most certainly the same.'

The day after his arrival Lasne determined, if possible, to gain the confidence of the Prince. Gomin gave up to him the daily care of the prisoner's clothes and cleanliness, and, though it was some time before the boy would answer his questions, Lasne gradually won his way. He introduced some slight improvements in the system of the prison. He even ventured to check Gourlet the turnkey

in the excessive noise he made every time the three
massive locks of the Prince's apartment were turned,
and desired him only to keep secure one of the doors,
the others being unnecessary. The turnkey obeyed,
but next day the municipal on duty sternly objected
to the smallest change in the rules, and Lasne was
silenced. Still he persevered in his effort to introduce
some cheerfulness into the gloomy place. He sang,
and encouraged Gomin sometimes to play the violin.
After three weeks' silence the boy at last spoke to
his new friend, and Lasne redoubled his attentions.
He told the sinking boy stories of the army, and of
the regiment which the boy had once commanded.
' Did you see me with my sword?' he asked in a
whisper, lest he should be overheard. The sword
exists still. It is in the collection of the Louvre, and
bears the simple inscription, ' Sword of the son of
Louis XVI.'

But the boy was sinking fast. On the 2nd of May
Lasne and Gomin thought it their duty to enter in
their daily report, ' The little Capet is ill.' No notice
was taken of the warning, and next day they wrote
again in the register of the Temple, ' The little Capet
is dangerously ill.' On the third day they added,
' There is danger of death.' On the 5th of May they
were informed that the eminent physician, M. Desault,
was to visit their prisoner. M. Desault examined his
patient long and anxiously, but the boy would not
answer his questions. The physician ordered for him
decoctions of hops, to be taken every half-hour during
the day. To the guardians M. Desault expressed no
opinion of the young King's state, but he informed
the Executive that he had been called in too late,
and he proposed that his patient should be removed
to country air. No measures however were taken in

accordance with his advice. On the 30th of May, as Desault was leaving the Temple, Breuillard, the municipal on service, said to him, 'The child is lost, is he not?' 'I fear so, but there are, perhaps, in the world persons who hope it.' Desault did not again visit the Prince. Next day the municipal on duty happened to be one Bélanger, an architect and painter, who had in former times been in the employment of 'Monsieur,' the young King's uncle. When he found Desault did not arrive at the usual hour, he went up to the prisoner's room saying that he would there await the doctor. He opened his portfolio and amused the Prince with the sketches in it, which for some time occupied the sick boy. Presently Bélanger asked if he might add another drawing to his collection. The Prince assented with a smile, and Bélanger drew, in crayon, the outline of his features. It was from this portrait that two busts of Louis XVII. were executed, one within a few days of Bélanger's visit by M. Beaumont, a sculptor, and, twenty years later, another, in the Sèvres manufactory of porcelain. It is difficult to understand how the fact of Bélanger's testimony is met by those who maintain that Louis XVII. had left the Temple a year before ; so difficult that another theory of the prisoner's evasion was invented to meet the exigency. It is pretended that Bélanger was an instrument employed by Monsieur to get his nephew out of the Temple, that Desault was never allowed to reappear, lest he might perceive the substitution— that he was poisoned at a dinner given to him by 'the Conventionals,' and that his notes of the young King's case were never forthcoming. In short, some mystery-mongers insist that Desault was sacrificed to some secret of the Temple. Yet, according to the *Biographie Medicale*, the *post-mortem* examination of

Desault showed no trace of poison. Bichat, his pupil, speaking of the rumour, observes, 'What illustrious man is there whose death has not been made a subject of false guesses by the public, which is ever ready to find in it something extraordinary?'

But whether Desault's sudden attack of malignant fever were the result of poison, or not, administered by Monsieur or administered by the Conventionnels, how are we to imagine that a dying boy was deftly exchanged for another, who, if not dying, was in a state of extreme prostration? Was the transfer effected in Bélanger's portfolio? Were the three guardians privy to the fraud as well as an indefinite number of officials and sentries? Was a boy found in a parallel state to the young King's, and ready to act his part of dying, while the miserable wreck of the Temple succeeded in active and difficult flight; and, finally, what definite advantage to Monsieur, or to the Convention, lay in the escape of the prisoner?

Nothing, on the other hand, can be more consistently probable than the events that really did take place, when we remember the confusion, and corruption, and terror of the time. A summary of the chief events that coincided with the time of the young King's last illness and death, will enable us to understand what in other times would seem suspicious in the treatment of a Prince, so important by birth.

The Republic had been successful abroad, and feared little from the Coalition. The Peace of Bâle on the 5th of April, and the Treaty of the Hague on the 16th of May, gave external security to the revolutionists. In the space of seventeen months France had gained twenty-seven battles, and had taken a hundred and sixteen fortified places; the attitude of Europe, therefore, left the Paris Executive free in its dealings with the 'little Capets,' and we have seen that the leaders of the Convention were not men to initiate any amelioration in the captivity of the ' tyrant's children.' In judging of the evidence we possess of Louis XVII.'s illness and death in the Temple, it is uncandid to cavil over some trivial informalities in the records of his end, and to draw important consequences from some omission there may chanced to have been in official routine. The state of Paris will account for more than the alleged deficiency in the proof of the Temple prisoner's identity with the son of Louis XVI. For instance, on the 27th of May, while Desault was administering his hop decoctions to the Prince, the Insurrection which has been called ' of Hunger,' threatened the existence of the Convention, and the head of Féraud was paraded before his fellow-deputies in their room of Assembly by a furious mob. Paris was the battlefield of Jacobins and Thermidorians. For two days the struggle of the factions continued, and then came terrible revenge on the conquered Jacobins. The remaining members of the old Executive, which had decided the fate of Louis XVII., were hunted down as wild beasts, and the trial of six among them, who had not escaped, filled men's minds, while the victim of the Temple languished to his grave. We do not easily conceive the fierce passions, the famine, and misery, the mad world of the ' White Terror,' but when once we get some idea of it, the neglect of the dying Prince appears a necessary result of the existing anarchy.

Even had it been practicable to remove him, it is doubtful whether any of the factions of the Emigration sincerely wished to liberate the ruined Prince. He was never likely, in his leadership, to satisfy their lust for revenge, or to prove a worthy master of the Œil de Bœuf. He had become useless to the royalists, and indifferent to the republicans. If there had been calculation in his treatment, it certainly had been successful in the double

M

destruction of his mind and body. Except in one or two, whose pity was roused by witnessing his condition, he could raise no interest or enthusiasm. Even in the memoirs of his sister may be traced a repugnance, which, as we have said, probably dated from the dreadful moment when, under the tutorship of Hébert and Simon, he had lied against his mother, and when his moral degradation must have been shamefully apparent.

, On the 17th of February, 1795, the chiefs of the Chouan revolt had made peace with the Convention, and it was said that among the secret articles of the treaty was one stipulating for the delivery to Charette of the son of Louis XVI. But the steady neglect shown to the boy by the Paris Government proved that such an ' article could only have been an hypocrisy. The days of the young King had been numbered, and his career for ever stopped, and, whatever the reaction of the nation towards royalty, Jacobinism had at least secured that the son of Marie Antoinette should be an object of contempt and incapable of government. The active regency of ' Monsieur,' meantime, rendered the life or death of his nephew of little political importance. Little interest, even among the courtiers of Verona, or the boon companions of the Comte d'Artois, was excited by the circumstances of the Prince's death in the Temple. The obscurity that closed around it was natural, and none but persons interested in the fortunes of some pretender, or greedy to cast discredit on the Bourbon restoration, need find a mystery in it.

The *Moniteur* of the day ascribed M. Desault's death to violent fever, brought on by excitement during the ' Insurrection of Hunger.' Five days passed before further medical aid was ordered for Louis XVII. ; days of such turmoil in Paris, that the tottering Government may well have been careless of the administration of frictions of hop decoctions to the dying boy. On the 5th of June, however, M. Pelletan, chief surgeon of a principal hospital in Paris, was sent to the Temple. 'I found,' he says, 'the child in so bad a state, that I urgently requested that another member of the profession should be associated with me, to relieve me from a burden which I could not support alone.' M. Pelletan at once ordered the removal of the window blinds, and the disuse of the noisy bolts, which, he observed, affected the patient's nerves painfully. 'If you do not at once do this,' he said emphatically to Thory, the municipal on service, 'at least you will not object to our carrying the child into another room, for we are, I suppose, sent here to give him proper care.'

The Prince then signed to him to come near, and whispered to him. 'Speak low,' he said, 'I fear lest they should hear you above, and I should be sorry that they knew I was ill, for it would give them great pain.'

It is said, by those who maintain that there was a substitute, that up to this the prisoner of the Temple had kept silence. They account for the fact of his having spoken to M. Pelletan, by declaring that a second substitute had replaced the dumb son of Baron Tardif, and they support the theory by pretending that the son of Louis XVI. must have known that his mother's apartment was too far off for the sound in his to reach her. But from Madame Royale's narrative, and from the depositions of the Prince against Madame Elisabeth, it is plain that noises in the second story had frequently been audible in the third. The recollection of his deposition weighed on him, and if he had brooded on his involuntary treachery, what more natural than his words to the surgeon?

He suffered much in the removal to the outer room, but we are told he never complained. M. Pelletan continued Desault's treatment, so, though no notes were left by Desault, it appears certain that both physicians thought alike of their patient. Neither of them was allowed to use the only efficient remedy, that of complete change. Even under M. Pelletan's care, the boy was obliged to remain alone from eight at night till eight in the morning, without a voice to cheer him in the valley of the shadow of death.

On the 6th of June he seemed slightly better. He took his medicine without repugnance, and Lasne helped him to get up. At half-past eight M. Pelletan arrived and examined him, but gave no new prescription. Towards two, Gomin went up with the prisoner's dinner, accompanied by the new commissioner of the day, who bore the ill-reputed name of Hébert. Lifting his head with difficulty from his pillow, the child took some spoonfuls of soup, and then lay down. Some cherries were put on the bed within his reach, and from time to time his shaking hand took up one, and he ate it with pleasure. 'So! so!' said Hébert, 'you shall show me, citizen, your order for moving the wolf cub out of his room.' 'We have no written order,' replied Gomin, 'but the doctor, whom you will see to-morrow, will tell you we have acted by his directions.' 'How long,' retorted Hébert angrily, 'has the republic been governed by barbers? You will have to ask leave from the Committee. Understand that!' Hearing the rough words, the boy left his cherries, and drew his hands slowly under the bed-clothes.

Next day M. Pelletan was informed that the Government had consented to associate a colleague with him. M. Dumangin, first physician of l'Unité, presented himself at the Temple on the morning of the 7th of June, with credentials from the Committee of Public Safety. Both doctors immediately went up to their patient.

They found him just recovering from a fainting fit, and
in a state of such prostration, that they both acknowledged that nothing could be done to restore his strength,
worn out by the long agony of imprisonment. They
expressed surprise at the solitude in which their patient
was left at night, and in their report were urgent for a
nurse. The Committee authorized the appointment of
any person as nurse who might be selected by the
physicians. But it was too late. Meantime, on the 7th,
the medical men withdrew, having done little more than
give permission that the dying boy might drink a glass of
sugared water if he complained of thirst.

At supper time, Gomin was surprized to find him
better; his eyes were brighter, his voice stronger, his
colour clearer. ' It is you!' he said to the guardian.
'So you suffer less,' said Gomin. 'Less,' replied the
child; but as he spoke a tear gathered and rolled down
his sunken cheek. Gomin asked him what was the
matter. ' Always alone,' the Prince murmured ; 'my
mother remained in the other tower.' Presently Gomin
said, ' It is sad, certainly, to be alone, but you are spared
bad company, and bad examples.' ' Oh, I see enough !'
answered the child ; ' but,' and he touched his guardian's
sleeve, ' I also see good people and they keep me from
hating the others.' ' N——,' continued Gomin, who in
reporting to ,M. de Beauchesne the conversation could
not recall the name, ' N——, who has often been here as
a commissioner, has been arrested, and he is in prison.'
'I am sorry,' said the child. ' Is he here?' 'No; in
La Force in the Faubourg S. Antoine.' 'I am sorry,'
said the Prince, after a long pause, 'I am sorry ; for you
see he is more unhappy than we are—he deserved his
misfortune." It has been said that no boy of ten could
have uttered so noble a sentiment. Louis the XVII.
had had strange teaching, and the clever child of

Versailles had been well grounded in high thoughts. It
is more likely that he should have spoken so, in the clear
hour that often heralds death, than that Gomin should
have invented the words.

Even on that last night his guardians were obliged to
leave him alone. Next morning, the 8th of June, Lasne
went up first to his room, for Gomin dreaded to find him
dead. At eight o'clock, when Pelletan arrived, the child
was up; but the physician saw that the end was near,
and did not stay many minutes. Feeling heavy and
weak, the Prince asked to lie down as soon as the doctor
was gone. He was in bed at eleven, when Dumangin
came; and with Pelletan's concurrence a bulletin was
signed, which announced the fatal symptoms of the
Prince's illness. He did not apparently suffer. Seeing
him quiet, Gomin said to him; 'I hope you are not in
pain just now.' 'Oh, yes, I still suffer, but much less;
the music is so beautiful.' Needless to say that there
was no earthly music in the Temple on that day!
'Where do you hear it?' asked Gomin. 'Up there;
listen, listen.' The child raised his hands, his eyes opened
wide, he listened eagerly, and then in sudden joy he
cried out, 'Through all the voices I heard my mother's.'

A second after, all the light died away in his face,
and his eyes wandered vacantly towards the window.
Gomin asked him what he was looking at. But the
dying boy seemed not to have heard, and took no notice
of the guardian's questions. After a time Lasne came
upstairs to replace Gomin. The Prince looked at him
long and dreamily, then on some slight movement of
his, Lasne asked him if he wanted anything. 'Do you
think my sister heard the music?' asked the child. 'It
would have done her good.' Soon after he turned his
eyes eagerly towards the window, a happy exclamation
broke from his lips, then looking at Lasne he said:

'I have a thing to tell you.' The guardian took his hand, the prisoner's head sunk on Lasne's breast, who listened in vain for another sound. There was no struggle, but when the guardian felt the child's heart, it had ceased to beat. It was a quarter past two o'clock in the afternoon.

CHAPTER XXIV.

Scattered dust.

INFORMED by Lasne that the young King was dead, Gomin and the commissioner of the day immediately went up to the room where he lay. They arranged the body, and lifted it to the inner chamber, where the child had spent his two years of suffering. Then the doors were thrown open for the first time since the republic had closed them on the 'tyrant's son.'

Gomin went without delay to the Committee of Public Safety. There he saw M. Gauthier, one of its members, who said, 'You have done well to come yourself and at once with the message; but it comes too late, and the sitting is over. The report of this cannot be made to-day to the National Convention; keep the news secret till to-morrow, until I have taken suitable measures. I will send to the Temple M. Bourguignon, one of the secretaries of the Committee of Public Safety, to assure himself of the truth of your declaration.' M. Bourguignon followed Gomin on his return to the Temple. He verified the event, renewed the recommendation of silence, and desired that the service should be carried on as usual. There is in these directions of M. Gauthier nothing to suggest mystery. It was a moment for the most measured prudence in individual members of the Government, when a false political step so easily cost a man his life, and when the dislocation of society and the universal suspicion were perhaps greater than during the Red Terror.

On the 9th of June, at eight o'clock, and therefore at the earliest moment possible to official form, four members of the Committee of General Safety came to the Temple to verify the Prince's decease. They affected extreme indifference. ' The event,' they said several times, ' has no importance ; the Commissioner of Police of the section will come to receive the declaration of death. He will verify it, and take measures necessary for burial without any ceremonies. The Committee will proceed to give the necessary orders.' When they were leaving, some officers of the Temple guard desired admission to see the remains of the little Capet. Damont, the commissioner on service, having observed that the guard would not allow the coffin to be taken out without requiring it to be opened, the deputies from the Committee decided that the officers and sub-officers of the day, and their reliefs, should be requested to verify the death of the boy. The two commissioners who were on service on the two following days were especially sent for, and, with their colleague of the day, remained in the Temple. Damont, by an order dated the day before, continued on service. Having collected the whole corps of the guard, he requested them to declare if they recognized the body as that of the ex-Dauphin. All who had seen the young Prince in the Tuileries or in the Temple attested that it was in truth the body of Louis XVI.'s son.

On their going down to the council-room, Darlot, one of the municipal commissioners, drew up formally the act of attestation. It was signed by some twenty persons, the names of ten of whom are given by M. de Beauchesne. The declaration was inserted in the register of the Temple, which after the liberation of Madame Royale was deposited at the Ministry of the Interior.

During these proceedings the surgeon directed to make the *post-mortem* examination arrived. MM. Pelletan and Dumangin chose as their assistants for the operation M. Lassus, who had been in attendance on the late King's aunts, and M. Jeanroy, who had been in the service of the house of Lorraine. The signatures of these gentlemen were, of course, particularly valuable under the circumstances. They went into the room where the body lay as soon as the officials of the Temple had finished their verification. M. Jeanroy observed that the bad light of the room was unfavourable to the accomplishment of their mission. The body was therefore removed to the outer chamber, and placed near the window, when the examination was made. Discredit has been cast on the evidence of the officials who saw the body while it remained in the inner room before M. Jeanroy's proposal was adopted. But there is a wide difference between the light required for a surgical operation and that which would be amply sufficient for a recognition of identity. The declaration of the four physicians has also been cavilled at. We confess that, taken in connection with their unvarying expression of belief in the identity of the prisoner—both at the time and after the Restoration—we see in the declaration only a formal and cautious assertion of the facts within the knowledge of the witnesses. In the first paragraph is set forth the decree of the Government directing them to carry out 'the *post-mortem* examination of the deceased Louis Capet's son.' In the second is the sentence which has been taken to express doubt, and which we beg our readers to note carefully: 'Having arrived at eleven o'clock in the morning at the external door of the Temple, we four were received by the commissioners, who took us into the tower. When we came to the second storey we found, in the second corner of the apartment, the dead body of a child, which appeared to be about ten years old. It was, the commissioners told us, the body of the son of the deceased Louis Capet, and two of us recognized it as the child for whom they had prescribed during some days. The same commissioner declared to us that this child had died the day before, towards three o'clock in the afternoon. We then endeavoured to verify the signs of death, which we found characterized by the general paleness, the cold habit of the body, the stiffness of the limbs, the glazed eyes,' &c. &c. In the declaration, which proceeds at length to detail the state of the body, there is only the careful elimination of all assumptions which is proper in' such documents and prudent in such a case. The anatomical description of the boy's condition concludes with the opinion of the examiners, that 'all the disorders of which we have given the detail are evidently the effect of a scrofulous tendency existing for a long period, and to which should be attributed the death of the child.' In 1817, M. Pelletan made a further declaration in which he asserts that he particularly examined the brain 'of the son of Louis XVI.'

Those who cling to the theory that Louis XVII. was stolen from the prison between the visits of Desault and Pelletan say that Desault's opinion of the prisoner's condition differed from that of his successor in the boy's care. The treatment of both physicians was, however, similar, and in the absence of Desault's notes, there is no trustworthy evidence of what his opinion was. It is remarkable that he attended the elder brother of the

Prince for the scrofulous disease of which he died, at Meudon, in 1789.

The National Convention received the report of the 'little Capet's' death with indifference.   It occurred at a moment of intense excitement in Paris—when the trial of the Jacobin deputies concerned in the ' Insurrection of Hunger ' was about to commence.   On the 11th of June, the news of the prisoner's decease was formally received by the Convention.   On the 12th began the proceedings that decided the future of the Republic ; for the safety of the Thermidorians depended on the destruction of Jacobinism as a principle in the persons of its leaders.   The disappearance of a dying child was of little moment in the struggle of parties.   The negligence and indifference of the Executive as to the Temple is not mysterious.   But if, at such a time, extraordinary exactness had been observed, and great publicity had been sought for the facts of the young King's death and interment, there would have been reason to suspect intrigue.

M. de Beauchesne has been able to give the public, by the kindness of the Duchesse des Cars, a letter from Madame de Tourzel, which shows that one of the persons most interested by affection in the Prince's fate was satisfied with the evidence of his death.

'Not able to endure the idea of a loss so painful to me,' writes Madame de Tourzel, 'and having some doubts of its reality, I wished to assure myself positively that all hope must be abandoned.   I had been acquainted from my childhood with the Doctor Jeanroy, an old man of eighty-four, of rare honesty, and profoundly attached to the royal family.   Being able to rely on the truth of his evidence as on my own, I sent to beg that he would visit me.   His reputation had caused his selection by the members of the Convention, that he might strengthen by his signature (at the foot of the declaration of the autopsy) the proof that the young King had not been poisoned. The good man had at first refused the proposal made to him to go to the Temple for verification of the causes of his death, warning them that if he perceived the slightest trace of poison he would mention it, even at the risk of his life. " You are precisely the man which it is essential for us to have," they said to him, "and it is for this reason that we have preferred you to all others."

' I asked Jeanroy if he had known him well before he came to the Temple. He said that he had seen him but seldom, and added, with tears in his eyes, that the countenance of the child, whose features the shadow of death had not changed, was so beautiful and interesting that it was constantly present in his thoughts, and that he should perfectly recognize the young Prince if he were shown his portrait. I showed him a striking likeness which I had fortunately preserved. " There can be no mistake," he said with tears, " it is himself, and no one could fail to recognize him."

' This evidence was further strengthened by that of Pelletan, who being sent for to my house in consultation some years after the death of Jeanroy, was struck by the resemblance of a bust which he found on my mantelpiece, to that of the dear little Prince, and though he received no hint which could have enabled him to recognize it, he exclaimed on seeing it, " It is the Dauphin, and how like him !". It was impossible for me to form the slightest doubt of the testimony of two such respectable persons, and there was nothing left for me but to weep for my dear little Prince.'

On the 10th of June, at six o'clock in the evening, a police commissioner and two civil commissioners of the section of the Temple, arrived at the tower to register the death of the prisoner, and take the body away for burial. M. de Beauchesne publishes a fac-simile of the form filled in by the officials. We confess that in it we see no trace of the carelessness which is alleged by the partisans of subsequent 'lost Princes.' It is a printed document fully filled up, certified by Dussert, the police commissioner, and attested by Lasne, Robin, and Bigot, who had been on service in the Temple at the time of the young King's death. At seven o'clock the body, which had been brought down to the courtyard, .after having been arranged in its coffin by the commissioners present, was taken to the Cemetery of St. Margaret. There was full daylight during the procession and interment. As there was a crowd of persons round the principal gate of the Temple, the commissioners proposed that the bier should be taken through a side door, but Dussert, who was in charge of all the arrangements, ordered it to be taken out by the main entrance. There, a small detachment of troops fell in as escort. Four men, who were relieved from time to time, carried the bier. A sergeant and six men preceded it, several officials and municipal commissioners followed, and after them a corporal and six men brought up the rear.

No mark was left in the burying-place to show the spot where the coffin had been placed. The soil was levelled, and about nine o'clock the official witnesses of the ceremony left the cemetery. Two sentries were stationed during the first nights, to prevent any person from meddling with the body. At ten o'clock of the same evening, a declaration that the decree of the Convention touching the burial of Louis Capet's son had been executed, was drawn up and signed by eight of the chief witnesses to it.

CHAPTER XXV

Relics.

IT has been made a subject of surprise that on the restoration of Louis XVIII., when the remains of Louis XVI. and Marie Antoinette were disinterred and honoured with splendid burial at St. Denis, no measures were taken to recover the relics of their son. On the motion of Chateaubriand, in January, 1816, the two Chambers had decreed that a monument should be raised to the memory of the royal victims of the Revolution, Louis XVII., Marie Antoinette, and Madame Elisabeth, and in the following February the King ordered search to be made for the remains of his unfortunate nephew. M. de Beauchesne gives the letter of the Prefect of Police, detailing, in June, the information which he had been able to collect from the police commissioner, Dussert, who had managed the Prince's funeral in all its arrangements, from Voisin, a grave-digger, attached to the cemetery at the time, and from the widow of one Valentin, who professed that her husband had transferred the coffin of Louis XVII. from the common pit to a private grave. From all the information obtained from these different persons (including the curé of St. Margaret), 'it results,' writes the Prefect, 'that the mortal remains of his Majesty Louis XVII., contained in a coffin of white wood, four feet and a half in length, were carried from

the Temple to the Cemetery of St. Margaret, towards
nine o'clock in the evening, and deposited in the large
·common pit; that a declaration of the ceremony was
·drawn up by the Sieur Gille, then police cortimissioner;
that it appears likely that the body was removed from
the common pit; that this operation was secretly
·executed during the same night or the following, by
Voisin or Valentin; that if it was done by the latter
the place where the ashes of the young King lie is
under the left pilaster of the church door; if by the
former, the private grave may be found in the spot which
Voisin has pointed out at the left of the cross raised in
the centre of the cemetery, on the back being turned
to the church.' Other witnesses declared that the funeral
·of the Prince had been only simulated, and that his
bones lay at the foot of the Temple tower, where he
had been a ̇prisoner; and the chief gardener of the
Luxembourg still further confused men's minds by a
long affidavit in June, 1816, to the effect that he had
·as he believed, aided to bury Louis XVII. in the distant
Cemetery of Clamart, in the presence of four members
·of the Committee of General Safety.

In the presence of so much uncertainty, and such con-
flicting reports, it is not surprizing that Louis XVIII.
hesitated to proceed in the identification of his nephew's
·ashes. Even about the comparatively easy verification
·of Louis XVI.'s remains there had hung doubt, which
·excited the scoffs of the enemies of the restored dynasty.
It would have been impossible to ·persevere in honouring
nameless dust, or sanctioning its intrusion into the vaults
of St. Denis, without such ridicule as might perhaps have
·endangered the lately regained crown. It was natural,
under the circumstances, that when the curé of St.
Margaret, with inconvenient zeal, made an application
to Madame Royale, then Duchesse d'Augoulême, that

her brother's remains might be sought for and placed in a chapel of his church, she should weep much, but refuse to order any search, 'because,' as she added, 'great care must be taken not to revive the memories of our civil discord, for the position of kings is terrible, and they cannot do all that they would.'

On the return of the Bourbons to power, M. Pelletan found it expedient to give out that, during the *post-mortem* examination of the prisoner in the Temple, he had taken away the heart. Lasne positively denied that such an important abstraction had been possible, but supposing that M. Pelletan had found means to carry away, at the risk of his life, to use his own words, the young King's heart, the subsequent history of the relic is altogether unsatisfactory. He declared that he had preserved it in spirits of wine, and that after ten years it became so dry that it could be put away in a drawer with other anatomical preparations. One day he perceived that it was gone, and his suspicion fell on a pupil, whom however he continued to receive in his house. M. Pelletan did not press for restitution lest the theft should be denied, and the relic destroyed. After the death of the young man his widow gave it back to M. Pelletan, who declared that he perfectly recognized it. He placed it in a crystal vase, on which were engraved the letters 'L.C.,' surmounted by seventeen stars and a lily, and the relic is still in the possession of the Pelletan family. Louis XVIII. had intended to place at St. Denis both M. Pelletan's relic and the heart of the eldest son of Louis XVI., which had been also, it was alleged, preserved by private loyalty, but the dread of fraud and mystification prevailed, and no measures were taken which might have roused a controversy.

The news of the unfortunate Prince's death spread rapidly through France, and failed not to suggest the most exaggerated rumours. It was said that he had been poisoned. The threats of more than one Conventionnel were remembered. People asked themselves, what were the 'useful crimes' of which deputy Brival had spoken when he regretted the presence of Capet's children in Paris? Cabot's advice that 'France should be delivered by the apothecary from Capet's son,' was recalled to mind; but there was no need of further violence than what the boy had already suffered, and there is no foundation for the stories of his having been poisoned by a dish of spinach or anything else. The *post-mortem* examination, and the verbal assertion of Desault, quoted by his friend M. de Beaulieu in his Essays on the French Revolution, set the question at rest. 'It appeared less dangerous to the republican chiefs,' wrote M. Hue, 'to labour for the destruction of all his moral faculties by ill-treatment, and to wear out his organs by terror, than to endanger their popularity by inflicting on the Prince a violent death.' 'If it happened,' calculated the tyrants of the clubs, 'that in any popular movement the people of Paris should visit the Temple to proclaim Louis XVII. King, we should show them a baby, whose stupid and imbecile appearance would force them to give up any project of placing him on the throne.'

'I do not believe that he was poisoned,' writes Madame Royale, 'as has been said, and is still said. The evidence of the doctors who opened his body proves it to be false, for they found not the slightest trace of poison. The drugs which he had taken in his last illness were analyzed, and found wholesome. The only poison which abridged his life was filth, joined to the horrible treatment, the cruelty, and severity without precedent, to which he was exposed.

N

The Regent 'Monsieur' did not delay to assume the rights which he inherited on the death of his nephew. He received the news at Verona on the 24th of June, and immediately announced his accession to the Courts of Europe. His proclamation to the French people was widely circulated throughout France, and on the 8th of July the Prince de Condé issued a violent manifesto to the emigrant army which concluded with the phrases, 'Gentlemen, the King Louis XVII. is dead. Long live the King Louis XVIII.!'

After the death of the Prince, his sister alone remained to embarrass the Convention. In various quarters some pity began to be felt for the imprisoned girl. More than one pamphlet was circulated in support of her liberation. But, while the heir of Louis XVI. lived, the Convention remained deaf to appeal. On his death there was little political capital to be made of Madame Royale. Austria offered two million francs as ransom for her, which were refused ; a public deputation from Orleans ventured to plead her cause, ineffectually indeed at the time, but the Government was sufficiently influenced to order that a list of what articles were necessary for the Princess should be made out. A lady to be her companion was selected, and she was permitted exercise in the court of the Temple. Gomin gave her a little dog, of ugly and low-bred aspect, but faithful and pleasant of manners. Madame Royale's health had borne well her long captivity, and the practice of self-control and self-reliance had left her singularly strong in spirit and dignified in demeanour. She had but one gown while in the Temple, a purple silk, but in her solitude she was always neat. Her chestnut hair, luxuriant in growth, was tied by a black ribbon, high on her head, and fell in curls behind. She had remained in ignorance of her utter orphanship, and the lady appointed to be her companion, Madame de Chanterenne, was obliged to break to her the news of the deaths of her mother, her aunt, and her brother.

'What, Elisabeth, too!' she exclaimed. 'For what was it possible to blame her? All is now over.'

Madame de Chanterenne succeeded in pleasing both the Princess and the Government, and she has left an official report in which she warmly praises the temper and disposition of her charge. Very soon the young girl resumed the tastes in which she had been early trained; she spent her time mostly in writing, reading, drawing, and needlework. Racine's and Boileau's works, and the letters of Madame de Sevigné and Madame de Maintenon were among the books she liked. She was glad to have some change of dress, though her toilet was as yet hardly royal. Linen and nankeen gowns, and on the greater festivals, a green silk, were her costumes in the Temple.

In September, 1795, the Duchesse de Tourzel and her daughter obtained leave to see the prisoner. They were surprized to find her so strong and well, and of such good courage. When they asked if she wished to leave France, she said, 'It is still some consolation to me to live in the country where are the remains of what is dearest to me in the world.' Then with tears, and in a lamentable voice, she exclaimed, 'Happier for me to have shared my parents' fate than to be doomed to sorrow for them.'

'I could not,' Madame de Tourzel says, 'help asking Madame how, sensitive as she was, she could have borne so many toils in such fearful solitude. Her answer was so touching that I transcribe it,' continued Madame de Tourzel. '"Without religion it would have been impossible; that was my only resource, and it gave me the sole comfort to which my heart was open. I had kept the religious books of my aunt Elisabeth. I read them, and thought over her advice; I tried not to deviate from it, but to follow it exactly. When she kissed me for the last time, she desired me particularly to ask that I might have a woman near me. Though I greatly preferred my solitude to the companion I should have been given at that time, my respect for my aunt's wishes obliged me to obey them. I was refused a companion, and I confess I was glad. My aunt only too well saw the difficulties before me, and she had accustomed me to wait on myself and do without any help. She had arranged my life so that all its hours were employed. The care of my room, prayer, reading, all my occupations were regulated. She had accustomed me to make my bed by myself, to do my hair, dress myself, and, besides, she had taken care for all that concerned my health. She taught me to sprinkle water about that the air of my room might be sweetened, and she required me to walk very fast, watch in hand, for an hour every day, that I might have the exercise I required." '

Though necessarily a centre of attraction, and to a certain extent, of intrigue, to the reviving royalists, Marie Thèrese was politically unimportant, and as soon as the negotiations for her exchange were completed she was handed over to the Austrian Government in return for the officials given up to Austria by Dumouriez, and for two republican envoys arrested by the Imperialists in Italy. On the 18th of December, 1795, at half-past eleven at night, and preserving a strict incognito under the name of Sophie, she left the Temple on foot, leaning on the arm of M. Benezech, then Minister for Home Affairs. She took her place at the Austrian Court, but her French attendants and friends were not favourably received, and in 1798 she joined her uncle at Mittau. Henceforth the story of her difficult and troubled life belongs to another page

of history, but the echo of those thoughts which preserved her in the thirteen months of her solitary captivity
was still audible in words used by her in 1842, and of
which the manuscript in her own writing still exists.

'Let us thank God for evil as for good! What though
we have loss in this world, we ought, like Job, to repeat
with humble resignation, "The Lord gave and the Lord
hath taken away! Blessed be His holy Name!" Every
day of our earthly life may be marked by suffering.
Let us lift up our souls to the Sovereign and Eternal
Good. May the Lord grant His infinite mercy to us
and to all those who have caused our sorrow.

'MARIE THERESE.

'March 4, 1842.'

In 1850, though slightly bent, she had still the firm
countenance and incisive speech of her early womanhood, and bore a strong likeness to Louis XVI. Three
times she was exiled from France, and three times she
witnessed the success of revolution and the fall of the
French monarchy. Yet she did not forget the lessons of
forgiveness and noble courage to endure which had been
taught her by those royal victims of a corrupt and selfish
past, her parents and her aunt.

After Madame Royale's departure from the Temple the
precautions used in guarding it were of course abandoned. Persons interested in the royal family contrived
to visit the rooms they had occupied, and have recorded
the inscriptions found in them. None were by the King's
hand or by that of Madame Elisabeth. There was in the
Queen's only a memento of her children's heights. In
the embrasure of her bed-rooms she had written in pencil,
27 mars quatre pieds, dix pouces, trois lignes; and lower
down, *Trois pieds, deux pouces.* In the Dauphin's room

were found two traces of his presence. He had drawn a flower on the wood-work near the corner, where the stove had been ; and further on, on another panel, these words were written with a badly-pointed pencil or a bit of charcoal—*Maman je vous pr——*

Madame Royale had left many tokens on the walls of her apartment. When the Conventionnel Rovère was afterwards imprisoned there he found written by her in pencil, *O mon Dieu, pardonnez à ceux qui ont fait mourir mes parents.* 'Remorse,' says Rovère, 'drove me from the room.'

There were many inscriptions by other hands in the apartments that had been occupied by the royal family. Old insults of the Jacobin era mingled with words of piety and sorrow. Below a sketch of *L'Autrichienne à la danse*, was written at a later date, *Regina martyrum, ora pro nobis ;* and across a rough design of a guillotine with the words, *Le tiran crachant dans le sac*, was written, *Celui que vous injuriez ici a demandé grâce pour vous sur son échafaud.*

During the Directory the tower of the Temple was used both as a barrack and a house of detention. It was to have been sold when Bonaparte came to supreme power as first consul, but he stopped the sale, and ordered it to remain a police barrack. As Emperor he learned to dislike the gloomy monument of Bourbon sufferings and Jacobin excesses. In June, 1808, the building was dismantled, and in the following October the materials of the old citadel of the Templars were sold for 33,100 francs to a speculator. He had hoped to enrich himself by the exhibition of the tower and its apartments, but the Government quickly stopped his appeal to Parisian curiosity. No persons except the labourers actually employed were allowed inside the buildings. The palace that had been attached to the

ancient sanctuary was in 1811 restored and furnished as
the official residence of the Minister of Public Worship.
After the return of the Bourbons it was occupied by a
religious congregation founded by Louis XVIII., at the
head of which was the former Abbess of Remiremont,
Louise Adelaide de Condé. A weeping willow and
some shrubs and flowers were planted where the tower
had been, and until 1848 a wooden railing inclosed the
spot. In 1853, the palace itself was taken down, and
and with it the last fragment of the mass of buildings
called the Temple disappeared. Yet the events that
have for ever made the place notorious do not sink out
of our sight as do other spectres of history. The sufferings endured there belong to our present time. The
revolution exists now as it did then. The same errors
lead men astray now as then, and the same results are
constantly possible. It is true that the revolutionary
doctrines now seem less startling, but it is because they
are more widely spread. The sophisms that wrought the
outburst of passion in 1789 are now commonly received
as truths. The carnage of the Terror with its open
vioation of law was indeed less dangerous than the
insidious displacement of justice by 'public opinion,'
which excuses the revolutionists of to-day. But the
'principles' of '89 are the principles still invoked;
the age that was begun by Voltaire and his followers
the Hébertists, by Rousseau and his disciple Robespierre, is ours. Ours is the society that outraged Marie
Antoinette and Elisabeth, ours the pre-eminent crime of
the child-King's demoralization and ruin; and if we
claim credit for the material improvement of our epoch,
we must also bear the shame of its unequalled and
mean cruelty—cruelty that always marks false Liberal-
ism, whether it be shown to a royal family dethroned,
or to a pauper in a workhouse.

But while we have in the history of the Temple a lesson of what political crime can be, while its annals register the worst form of revolutionary injustice yet seen in our society, they contain also the record of a faith and courage, a patience and power of forgiveness, that has never been surpassed in our time. If we justly dread the red spectre of the Terror, we should gather consolation from the white-robed forms which beckon us across its glare to the place of divine order and law, that was, and is, and shall be ever the same and immutable—a haven for those who are not beguiled by the fallacies of revolutionary progress. Among the heroic figures that lead us through the storms and fogs of this present world back to a more Christian tme may be reckoned even the weakly and blasted child of the Temple. Victim of cruelty, incomprehensible to him, a prey to torture which no other child was ever called to endure, nearly his last words were those, solemnly attested by Gomin, of goodwill to the municipal who had ill-treated him ; of patience, faith, and hope, when he prayed his guardian to be consoled in the sight of his sufferings, '*For*,' said the boy, '*I shall not always suffer.*'

Yes, there is mystery in his history—the mystery of great crime, and the mystery of a child's resistance to crime. Speaking of her brother's death, Madame Royale writes, ' The commissioners sorrowed bitterly for him, he had so endeared himself to them by his loveable qualities.' Can we wonder that to those who do not believe in divine grace the endurance of the tortured Prince in faith, hope, and charity, should be an insoluble mystery? How could the patient and still noble child, that Lasne and Gomin loved, be the same as Simon's apprentice and Hébert's victim? Had not the prayers of his parents somewhat to do with the mystery of the Temple? Was not a guardian angel at hand, when the boy stayed the murderous hand of Simon by the words, '*I will forgive you*'?

But while confessing the crimes wrought at the bidding of atheistic sophistries, no thinker should neglect the lessons taught by that storm of electric emotion, lawless as only moral storms can be, that broke over Europe and struck down the royal family of France.

It was a fierce demand for what were possibly legitimate rights; but the fatal doctrine, that for public purposes and national safety the end justified the means, wrought more hideous anarchy than has been known since the Christian commonwealths were established on immutable justice.

To detect the social and ethical errors that would dethrone this justice, to return to the laws and customs. that have made Europe what it is, to repress crime by authority, not endeavouring to escape from it by experimental politics, and to restore the divine order of family life, is the cure for our modern social instability.

The story of the royal prisoners in the Temple is a forcible lesson in the virtues taught by the old Christian order. Had Louis and his wife never tampered with un-Christian error they would have left a yet brighter aureole around their names. Yet God has willed that in their very mistakes they should be profitable to those who will learn. Which of us readiest to blame their shortcomings could so valiantly have expiated them, and so nobly have carried the fatal burden of dynastic evil, even to the scaffold?

THERE have been and still are so many pretenders to be descendants of the unhappy son of Louis XVI., false Dauphins and false Louis XVII., and false Dukes of Normandy have been so rife that it seems well to conclude this sketch of the boy's life by the judgment of the Court of Appeal in Paris on the Naundorff case, which was delivered on the 28th of February, 1874. It sums up authoritatively the verdict of all unprejudiced Frenchmen, and as the eloquence and professional skill of M. Jules Favre had left no document untested, no source of evidence unexplored, the judgment may surely be taken as conclusive.

'The court enacts on the appeal lodged by Jeanne Frederique Einert, widow of Charles Guillaume Naundorff, and by the Naundorffs, husband and wife, his children, from the judgment delivered between them and Henri Dieudonné, Comte de Chambord, by the Tribunal of the Seine, bearing date 5th of June, 1851 ;

' Considering that the widow Naundorff and the children born of her marriage, claim, as against the Comte de Chambord, the position and rights which should belong to them as representing the son of Louis XVI., King of France ;

' Considering that Louis Charles, Duke of Normandy, son of the King Louis XVI., died in the tower of the Temple at Paris, the 8th of June, 1795, as has been declared in an authentic certificate of his death, dated the 12th of the same month (24 Prairial, year III.) ; that this certificate, which had been preserved in the archives of the Hotel de Ville of Paris, and which existed at the date of the judgment, was destroyed in 1871 with all the municipal archives in the conflagration by the Commune, but of which uncontroverted copies exist, and one of which was especially produced by the appellants in their preliminary writ of instance ;

' Considering that the certificate of death aforesaid was made out in due form and within lawful delay by the public officer, on the declaration of two witnesses, according to the law then in force of the 24th December, 1792 ;

' That the widow and heirs Naundorff, taking the name of Bourbon, pretend to offer contrary proof to the declaration of death contained in it, and demand that it shall be annulled ;

' That they maintain that the certificate applies to the death of a child unknown, who had been substituted in the prison of the Temple for the Dauphin of France, son of Louis XVI., and that the young Prince whose escape had been contrived was, under a borrowed name, Charles Guillaume Naundorff, their husband and father ;

' That it is in this case a question of rightly appreciating the worth of the proofs adduced on this point by the appellants, and the allegations in support of them ;

' Considering that the Dauphin and Marie Thérèse, his sister, were imprisoned, one on the second, the other on the third storey of the great tower of the Temple, which rose in the centre of the court called by the same name, that each of these storeys, served by stairs that filled a corner turret, were shut in by two massive doors in oak and in iron ; that the first storey, forming a vast arched hall, was used as guard-house, that in the only room also on the ground floor, called the Chamber of the Council, were posted officers of the municipality, while the guardians of the royal children slept there ;

' That these guardians, forbidden to absent themselves, were named by decrees of the Committees of " Salut public " and of " Sureté generale," chosen from the Convention ;

' That for increased security a municipal commissioner had been added to the permanent guardians, who was to be changed every twenty-four hours, and successively furnished by each of the forty-eight sections of the Commune of Paris ;

' That consequently the arrangement of the localities, the exceptional watchfulness, and the political precautions adopted by the revolutionary authority of the epoch, alike

placed obstacles in the way of an escape—no one could go
in or out of the prison without being several times subjected to the most vigorous inspection ;

'Considering that the pretended escape would have been
accomplished by a personal substitution, and that to explain
this substitution a most extraordinary narrative is offered ;

That according to the Naundorffs, husband and wife,
three successive substitutions were effected ; that first a
lay figure, brought in a basket, was substituted for the
Dauphin, and the Dauphin was hid under his bed in this
basket ; that afterwards the lay figure was replaced by a
dumb child, whom it was attempted to poison ; that this
attempt at poisoning having been stopped by the skill of
the doctor, a rachitic child, very ill, was substituted for the
dumb child, who died some time afterwards in the prison,
and to whom is applicable the certificate of death of the
12th June, 1795, which is made out in the name of the son
of Louis XVI. ;

'Considering that the mere enunciation of such a theory
already shows in what value it should be held by a court of
justice ;

'That it is plainly seen what has suggested the inventing
of the story ;

'That the most certain evidence having made known the
determination of the young captive to preserve obstinate
silence towards those who visited him, and a report made by
three members of the Convention having verified the silence
he opposed to all questions, the idea was entertained of
alleging that a dumb child was substituted for the Dauphin,
so as to make his escape more probable ;

'That, on the other hand, as it is also certain that the
child imprisoned in the Temple sank under the consequences
of the scrofulous affection, for which he had been medically
treated, and of which the *post-mortem* examination described
the symptoms, persons were also led to imagine the theory
of a rachitic scrofulous child at the point of death, who in
his turn took the place of the dumb substitute for the
Dauphin ;

'Considering that it would be necessary to admit, according to the general purport of this story, that on three different
occasions, notwithstanding the most strict watch, and one

least easily deceived, it was possible to introduce into the tower of the Temple and to the Dauphin's floor, the lay figures, the dumb and the rachitic child, and that subsequently, as is declared in a memorial of the appellants, the dumb, the rachitic, and the royal child, all three resided simultaneously in the tower, where, nevertheless, there was no place of concealment besides the three floors, of which mention has been made, except in the fourth storey, which consisted of one large room ;

'Considering that to support so improbable a tale it is suggested that Barras, yielding to the request of Josephine de Beauharnais, favoured the escape, and to this end had appointed Laurent guardian of the royal children ; that as principal basis for the suit three letters, attributed to Laurent, are produced, which confirm the facts of the substitutions and of the escape which ensued ;

'But considering that here is manifest fraud ;

'That according to the report of an honourable magistrate of the court of Metz, who was the friend and counsellor of Barras, this last always affirmed that the Dauphin son of Louis XVI. died at the Temple ;

'That the three letters attributed to the guardian Laurent are copies of which the originals are not forthcoming, and that there is even no means of making known how they cam into the Naundorffs' possession ;

'That evidently Naundorff could have fabricated these proofs at his leisure, and that it is frivolous to offer them as an element of proof ;

'That it has been vainly attempted to give them some consistency by arguments based on their perfect agreement with the visit aforesaid of the three Conventionnels to the Temple, and with the dates of the commissions as guardians which were given to Gomin and Lasne ;

' That it was easy for a fabricator of letters to get information on these latter facts, which were recorded in public documents ;

'That the clumsiness of the fabrication is betrayed by a particular indication ;

' That originally the published letters bore at their foot a signature in which Laurent was written with a final *s*, that as it was necessary to acknowledge this to be a mis-spelling it became advisable to say that the letters were unsigned, and that it had been a mistake to add a signature to them ;

'Considering, these letters being rejected, and the general tender of proof being examined, that except a very suspicious hearsay, the deponents have been unable to point out any of the numerous agents who were called on to cooperate outside the prison, whether in the three successive substitutions of which mention has been made ; whether in the pretended burial of a rachitic child in the garden of the Temple ; whether in, as is still related, the arrangement of a hearse on which a coffin containing the living Dauphin was placed, and in which a clever contrivance enabled the transfer of the Dauphin from the coffin into a chest on the way to the cemetery ;

'Considering that, therefore, in the proofs offered nothing relates to the actual fact of escape ;

'Considering on the contrary that a direct and absolutely convincing proof, negativing all this story of escape, results from the evidence of Gomin and Lasne, which was legally taken in 1834, 1837, and 1840 ;

'That Gomin and Lasne appointed as guardians of the Dauphin, by decrees of the Committees of the Convention, fulfilled their duties in the Temple—one, Gomin, from the 8th November, 1794, that is to say during seven months ; the other, Lasne, during two months and a half ;

'That both, old officers of the National Guard, who knew the Dauphin by having frequently seen him in the Tuileries garden before his imprisonment, were in a position to give a circumstantial account of his illness and death ;

'That both have declared that the young captive spoke to them, while to all others he persevered in his inflexible resolution of silence, so that it is impossible to conceive that the prisoner was a dumb child who had been substituted for the Dauphin ;

'That both certified in a manner equally positive to have seen the child that they recognized to be the Dauphin die in the Temple, and that under their eyes the autopsy of the body was made ;

'Considering that by the side of this evidence of the two official guardians of the State prison is to be placed the

attestation of the municipal commissioner Damont, called to
the Temple for his turn of service as associated guardian on
the 8th of June, 1795, the day of the Dauphin's death ;

'That a report of the 16th August, 1817, preserved in the
national archives, and which is signed by Damont, contains
the declarations following from him :

'Arrived at the Temple by noon he found the royal child
still alive, though seemingly in a hopeless condition. He
recognized him by having seen him before his imprisonment
walking in the little garden reserved for him at the end of
the terrace of the Feuillants.   The same day at the Temple
some officers and the guard-reliefs equally with him recognized the Prince in the child who had just breathed his
last ;

'Considering—what sets the seal to the demonstration—
that the story of the death of a rachitic child who had been
exchanged for the Dauphin, is shown to be false by a comparison of the following dates ;

'That according to the theory of the Naundorffs, husband
and wife, which is entirely based on Laurent's supposititious
letters, the rachitic child secretly brought in by liberators
was introduced into the Temple within the dates of the
5th February and the 3rd March, 1795, for Laurent's letter
of the 5th of February announces that a child who was very
ill was about to be substituted for the dumb child, and the
letter of the 3rd of March declares that the substitution is
effected ;

'Now it is to be observed that at this time Gomin, whose
nomination dates from the 8th of November, 1794, had for
three months fulfilled his duties at the Temple ;

'That, therefore, it was while Gomin was guardian that
the pretended substitution of the rachitic child was carried
out, and that, therefore, Gomin must necessarily have been
an accomplice in the escape if he allowed the rachitic child
to take the place of the child, whoever he was, who had
been during the preceding three months in his charge, but.
that this supposition of Gomin's complicity could not be.
advanced ;

'That no one ever ventured to suggest it ;

'That it would contradict the whole theory of the Naundorffs', based on the assertion that Laurent had been

appointed guardian for the purpose of the evasion, and
that he left the charge of the young prisoner to Lasne and
to Gomin, "a republican in whom," according to his first
letter, "he had no confidence," only when the success of the
plan of escape was assured ;

'Considering, to express a final conclusion, that even if the
serious evidence of Lasne and Gomin, given before a magistrate by honest and disinterested old men attesting facts
long after the event, might have been criticized in its details,
the main points could not be doubtful ; that they are con-
firmed by Damont, that they are consistent even with
Naundorff's fraudulent document, and that, agreeing with
the general sense of the facts, they place above all attack the
truth of the certificate of the Dauphin's death ;

' That if the moral proofs be alone weighed this truth at
once suggests itself if it is borne in mind that the royalist
party, necessarily informed, would have drawn large advan-
tages from the deliverance of the Dauphin at a time when
the Vendéan war was active, also that devoted efforts would
not have been wanting to provide that the continuator of
the dynasty under the name of Louis XVII. should escape
an existence of obscurity, of ignoble abandonment, of
miserable adventure, of danger and of misery ;

' Considering that the truth of the certificate of death
being established, there is no need to dwell on pleas deduced
from a number of vague rumours, of futile presumptions, of
deductions guessed at, and of some worthless claim to
foreign status, by the help of which it has been attempted
to show the identity of Naundorff with Louis XVII., the
supposed survivor of the Temple captivity;

' That when the principal points in Naundorff's history
are summed up, . . . it is impossible but to see in him a
bold adventurer . . . ;

' Considering that from all that precedes it follows that
the disputed certificate of the death of Louis Charles, Duke
of Normandy, son of Louis XVI., the King of France, has
all the weight of authenticity, and that the allegations in
disproof of its declarations should be rejected as disproved
by existing testimony, and contrary to a demonstrated
truth ;

' Considering finally that this judgment only accords so full an examination of motives, and one possibly beyond what is fitting to the character of the suit, in order that the barriers of justice may be the higher raised against the audacious attempt to usurp a royal name and to falsify history ;

' On these grounds ;

' And, moreover, adopting those taken by the first judges, the court gives judgment by default against the Comte de Chambord, who has not appeared by attorney ;

' Gives a certificate to the appellants that they have renewed the instance pending on their appeal ;

' And, without pausing to consider the new inferences alleged in proof of the Naundorffs, husband and wife, which are rejected ;

' Annuls the appeal ;

' Confirms the judgment which non-suited the widow Naundorff and her children ;

' And condemns them in costs.'

The ' Mystery of the Temple' may remain an interest to some minds, curious of historical tangles, and glad to show shrewdness by demanding extraordinary proofs such as are seldom forthcoming in human affairs, but to all others the Dauphin's death will be as certain as any event can be that was so shrouded in gloom and social confusion.